For Matthew

And

Angels We Never Knew

# The Last
# Station Master

# The Last Station Master

## A BOY, A TERRORIST, A SECRET, AND TROUBLE

## S.A.M. POSEY

KPH

The Key Publishing House Inc.

First Edition 2013
The Key Publishing House Inc.
Toronto, Canada
Website: www.thekeypublish.com
E-mail: info@thekeypublish.com
ISBN 978-1-926780-22-1
eISBN 978-1-926780-47-4

Cover design and typesetting by Narinder Singh

Printed and bound in USA.

Published by a grant and in association with The Key Research Center (www.thekeyresearch.org). The Key promotes freedom of thought and expression and peaceful coexistence among human societies.

KPH

The Key Publishing House Inc.
www.thekeypublish.com
www.thekeyresearch.org

# Acknowledgements

My many thanks to friends, family, and writers of kindred spirit who supported this project and gave so generously of their time.

# Table of Contents

# 1
# BUSTED

N ate drummed his thumb on the steering wheel, watching the rearview mirror as the man approached. "We need to bounce."

"Are you kidding?" Malcolm whispered from the passenger seat. "How hard would it be for them to trace this car to me?" Sweat beads on Malcolm's forehead and his wild dreads wouldn't help their situation.

"Fine." Nate buttoned his polo shirt, hoping the Boston Preparatory logo embroidered on the front, along with his clean-cut looks, would earn them a pass. "Just let me do the talking." He straightened in the seat and rolled down the window.

The noise and fumes of passing motorists drifted into the car. Rush-hour traffic slowed with gawking drivers. He would give anything to be one of them right now instead of the middle-aged white cop's focus of attention.

The cop stopped two feet away with a pad in one hand and clicked a pen with the other.

"When an officer of the law signals you over, you pull over."

"Sorry, officer. I didn't think you meant me. I don't remember doing anything wrong back there."

The man pointed the pen at the rear of the car. "You have a tail light out. That could be a problem, especially if the other one goes too. I'm going to need your license and registration."

"Ah man, for a busted tail light?"

"The ticket is for not complying with an officer, otherwise we would be looking at a warning."

"But I *did* pull over," Nate reminded him.

"License and registration," the cop repeated.

"Yeah, okay." Nate leaned over and shuffled through papers inside the glove compartment of the red Mustang, wondering what a registration looked like. He pulled out a square slip of paper with the make and model of the car typed across it. He passed it to the cop and hoped he had guessed right. Boston's finest scrutinized the paper with a frown.

"Name on this registration says Angela Epson."

"Right, she's a neighbor."

"So this is her car?"

"Yes, sir."

"If I called her, she would verify you have permission to drive it?"

"Well, you can try calling, but she's out of town so you won't reach her at home. Sorry, I don't know the number of her cell."

"Let's have a look at your license, son."

*Busted.* "Oh, yeah, well, see…" Nate started. The explanation seemed reasonable when they first got the idea, but now he wondered if it sounded lame. "I'm supposed to get my permit on Monday, but we didn't think anyone would mind us taking a trial run. Right now, I don't actually have a permit, but I will in a couple of days."

The cop blew out a sigh. "Step out of the car, son. You too, kid," he told Malcolm. "We're taking a little trip to the station."

They exited the Mustang and were handcuffed then guided into the backseat of the police cruiser for a five-minute trip downtown.

Through a hall crammed with people, the cop kept a tight grip on their forearms until they reached a booth.

"I got two juvies on a joyride, Frank," the cop told the man standing behind a tall desk.

Frank acknowledged the cop with a nod. "Sorry, Bill. They get low priority. Our hands are full today. Cuff them over there until I can process them." Frank nodded to a wood bench in a corner.

"You got it," cop Bill said. "They can wait."

"Actually, my parents are sort of waiting for me," Nate said.

"Don't worry. We will be calling them."

Nate slumped onto the bench next to Malcolm as the cop walked away. "I can't believe this."

"Sorry, man," Malcolm said. "This is my fault."

"Don't worry about it," Nate said. Malcolm had meant well. If not for the cop profiling them, they wouldn't be here.

"I got to, man. My dad's going to kill me." Malcolm lifted his face to the ceiling like he wanted to howl or maybe plea for divine intervention. "Remember how he lost it when he caught us drinking his beer?"

"Yeah, that was more like a nuclear meltdown." He was ready to tease Malcolm about being toast and how it had been nice knowing him when he noticed a muscle-bound white dude watching them from across the hall. The dude wore black jeans and a T-shirt with a skull on the front. He had tattooed biceps Hells Angels would envy. The man tugged the cap he wore and headed over.

"Say, are you Independent Daniel's kid?"

"Um, yeah." Nate squinted to make out the man's features, shadowed beneath the bib of the cap.

"Boy, you've grown. You're the spitting image of Inde; you know that? How's he doing?"

"Yeah, he's good," Nate said and turned away, hoping the guy would go get in someone else's face. If he got out of this, he didn't need a witness who knew his dad.

"So, where is he?" The man's gaze swept the room before noticing the handcuffs that bound them to the bench. "What are you boys up to?"

Before Nate could think of a lie, Malcolm blurted out the truth.

"It's like this, see. I was house-sitting for a neighbor who has this maxed-out Mustang. It's my bro's here birthday so I didn't think it would hurt to take a quick spin. See, we didn't know it had a busted tail light and then this cop started acting like we were hardcore gang members or something." Malcolm finally took a breath; Nate felt like he needed one too. Malcolm was his boy but sometimes he had all the cool of a bonfire.

The guy frowned. "You're waiting to be booked?"

"Yeah, see, that's messed up, right?" Malcolm said.

"Hmm, hold here, I'll check it out."

"Yeah, cool. We'll wait," Malcolm said as if they had a choice.

Nate figured the man suffered from a distorted opinion of his own importance. He didn't get his hopes up, but the guy came back thirty minutes later with news.

"We've located the owner." He shook his head. "You're lucky Ms. Epson isn't pressing charges, but she's disappointed in you boys."

"Yeah, we're really sorry." Malcolm's eyes sparkled more with relief than remorse. "So if there're no charges, we can bounce, right?"

"You two had no business driving the car. You will have to face some consequences for that." The man pulled a key from his pocket and unlocked their cuffs.

"Yeah, thanks." Nate rubbed his wrist. "But can't you tell us what we can do to fix this? We don't need to involve our parents, right?"

The man shook his head and laughed. "Come on, I'll drive you home."

Ten minutes after delivering Malcolm into his dad's clutches, the man pressed the lighted button on the doorbell at Nate's house. His mom answered.

"How's it going, Saite?" he greeted her.

"Jimmy, my goodness. It's been awhile. Come on in here." For a moment, Nate held the thinnest hope that the reason for the escort home would get lost in reunion talk.

Dad sat in an armchair but stood to shake Jimmy's hand. "I hear it's Detective James Shore now. Got a nice ring to it, man. Congratulations on the promotion. Have a seat."

"Nah, I can't stay, Inde." Detective Shore took off his cap and ran his large hand through his blond hair. "I wanted to drop off Nate. He and Malcolm Lee were pulled over downtown on Tremont."

"Pulled over?" Mom frowned. "For what?"

"Joyriding. The owner isn't pressing charges, but there is the matter of the fine plus an impound fee for the car."

That's when Mom and Dad turned on him, throwing questions but not pausing to let him answer. Detective Shore's voice burst through the chaos and saved him from the verbal bombardment.

"Look, guys, I'll leave your boy to explain, I should get going."

"Jimmy." Mom blinked back tears then took a deep breath. She tiptoed to kiss the detective's cheek. "Thanks so much."

Dad sighed and shook the man's hand again. "Thanks, Jim."

"Not a problem." Detective Shore put his cap on then aimed a stone cold glare at Nate that could scare the statues off Easter Island. "Stay out of trouble."

Nate swallowed and leaned back a little. "Yes, sir."

Dad walked the detective to the door then returned and dropped into an armchair, studying him without saying a word. On the flip side, Mom transformed into a Tasmanian devil.

"Nathan Freedman Daniels!" She put a hand on her hip and shifted her weight to one foot. "You stole a car? Are you insane?"

He shot a HELP look to Dad because Tasmanian devils often ate their young.

"Let's give the boy a chance to explain, honey."

"Inde—" Mom started.

"Saite," Dad interrupted, "we have company." He nodded to Ell.

Nate's best friend since childhood sat quietly on the corner of the couch, but Ell was more like a sister than company. Presents on the coffee table in front of her caught his attention, as did the scent of chocolate angel food cake wafting through the air. The smell made his mouth water because the cake was his favorite and he hadn't eaten since lunch. He hoped his parents would wait until after his B-day celebration to lecture him.

"Don't even think about it, Nate," Dad said as though reading his mind. "Those presents will go back to the store, and I think we need to cancel dining out and the movie, don't you agree?"

*No, not really.* Nate wanted to say, but this wasn't a punishment to haggle over. "Okay, but it's dark outside. Can I see Ell home?"

"All right," Dad said. "But get back here fast."

"Sure." Nate stood, grateful for a chance to escape and give his parents a chance to cool off. "Come on, Ell."

At the bottom of the stoop, they cut across the grass to the brownstone Ell shared with her mom next door. A dim porch light illuminated pots of orange marigolds lining their front steps.

"Man, I can't believe I'm not getting anything for my birthday." He turned to Ell, expecting a little sympathy.

"How about I print you a 'get out of jail free' card?" she said "Should I wrap it in a ribbon?" He kept forgetting how much like his mom she was. She rolled her eyes. "You were totally wrong, Nate."

"See, I don't understand how Mom does it. I mean, does she channel herself through you or what?" He leaned over to give her skinny five-foot-two frame a hug. "Stop lecturing me. You're my girl, right?" he teased and tugged at her dark-brown curls to get her to chill. Instead of giving him the usual punch to the shoulder, she blushed beneath her pale Latino skin. Ell was getting harder to read all the time. Lately, just meeting her eyes caused her to blush. Something was happening with her.

"Ell, w'sup?"

She took a breath like she needed to calm down. "I want to tell you …" She stopped then hunched her shoulders and smiled. "It'll wait." That was Ell. Her mood could turn on a dime. Ten years of friendship had taught him it was never any use trying to pry more out of her.

He nudged her shoulder. "I always got your back. You know that, right?"

"Yeah, I know." Her face went all goofy before she dodged past him and ran up the steps then into the house.

Once more, he wondered what was up with his best friend then scratched his head and walked home.

His parents waited in the living room with expressions so serious, they could intimidate a Third World tribunal.

"Sit, Nathan." Mom was seated on the arm of Dad's chair. "Do you have any explanation for what happened today?"

"Sure, we just borrowed Malcolm's neighbor's car."

"So Malcolm's neighbor gave two fifteen-year-olds permission to drive a car?" she said in a 'what kind of sense does that make' tone.

"Not exactly; she wasn't there, but Malcolm said she wouldn't mind."

"Son." Dad pinched the bridge of his nose. "We expect you to mess up at times, but we also expect you to know where to draw the line. From the number of mess-ups you've gotten into lately, it's obvious you do not. That forces your mom and I to consider options that will help you understand how bad decisions have serious consequences. Here is what we're going to do." Dad pinned him with a penetrating stare. "School lets out for summer in a few days. You're going to spend some time with your grandparents to reflect on your recent choices."

*Wow!* He wanted to jump with joy. *This was his punishment?* "Okay, I'll do a summer in New York," he said, hoping to sound put upon. Dad's parents lived in New York. The last family reunion there had been a blast.

"No, not your father's parents." Mom sounded exasperated. "*My* parents."

His cheeriness vanished. "You're kidding, right?"

"Hardly," she answered flatly.

"Yeah, all right," he agreed like he had options. "But I don't think I need a whole summer. How about a week?"

"The whole summer," Dad's no-negotiation voice thundered and made it clear that this was final.

Mom's parents never talked about their life in North Carolina when they came for visits. They probably didn't want to bore people to death. Although Nate had never visited them, he knew they lived miles from any neighbors. He could forget about the Internet too, because their technophobia made exceptions for only a phone and a TV without cable or satellite. This would be the worst two months of his life.

# 2
# FLIGHT 417

Nate gazed past the empty window seat to the terminal. Security precautions put in place after Nine-Eleven excluded friends and family from the departure gates. Not getting a chance to wave a last goodbye was making him miss his parents and Ell even before the plane left the runway.

The pilot's intercom voice announced Delta Flight 417 would be nonstop to North Carolina. A flight attendant went through the 'What to do if this plane crashes routine'; which, he thought, would at least be an adventure.

A boy and a girl about his age were in the seats across the aisle from him. The boy sat by the window and wore a black knit cap and earphones from an iTouch. The girl was hot enough to throw lava balls and not be burned. She was working on one of those friendship bracelets Ell and her girlfriends wore. He forced his gaze away, but it kept wandering back to her. When she caught him checking her out, he grabbed the Fly Mall magazine from the seat in front of him and buried his face in the pages.

He continued faking interest in the magazine, but he noticed how the girl still watched him. He tugged his collar and pretended to read an article on Turtle Island as the girl reached over to shake hands.

"Hi, I'm Hannah," she said and flashed a dazzling smile.

His brain short circuited. "Oh, ah…" His face burned. "What?" He forgot his name. "Yeah," he mumbled then scooted over to the window and stared out at the clouds. Nope, the Casanovas of the world had nothing to fear from his game.

Two long hours passed with him crammed into the window seat, pretending fascination with the view of the clouds at 36,000 feet. At last, the pilot announced the plane was making an approach to the airport. Nate ignored the buckle-up sign and jumped up to pull his bag from the overhead compartment. He dropped back into the seat as a Barbie-doll looking attendant headed over, giving him the evil eye.

The attendant reached him and shook her head. "Sorry," he mouthed and gave her one of his stupid-kid smiles.

"We have rules in place for your safety. You must stay in your seat until the buckle-up sign is off."

"Yeah, I'm really sorry." He tried another smile; afraid she would take his bag and shove it back into the overhead compartment to make her point. Sometimes grown-ups did stuff like that. But maybe the smile worked this time because the attendant rolled her eyes and walked away.

The plane taxied onto the runway, and he hauled into the aisle before a friendly voice from the audio system could finish the 'Thanks for flying Delta Airlines speech.

Several passengers stood too, blocking his way. A minute passed and no one moved any closer to the exit. Someone tugged the sleeve of his hoodie from behind. He turned just as a flight attendant with almond-shaped eyes squeezed past him.

"We apologize for the delay, but we must ask everyone to return to their seat." She ruffled the white shirt and tie he was wearing to impress his grandparents as she passed, repeating the same vague message to the passenger ahead of him. The people behind him must have gotten the same request because most were returning to their seats or already sitting and looking anxious.

He lingered a few moments more, wondering what was up. Then the pilot's microphone voice announced, "Ladies and gentlemen." Right away, he knew something really was up. No one said 'ladies and gentlemen' unless they wanted you to behave that way. "We have been asked to hold our position on the tarmac until security arrives."

*Security?* His mind jumped immediately to terrorists. Waiting for security seemed like a stupid idea. Logic dictated that everyone beat a quick path to the exit. Unfortunately, the flight attendants had positioned themselves to prevent that.

"Everyone remain calm," a tall white man with a beer gut bellowed as he pushed his way down the aisle, forcing people to take whatever seats were available as he passed. He seemed like someone used to being in charge. Probably one of those air marshals the government started putting on planes after Nine-Eleven.

Nate decided to retreat to his seat before the air marshal reached him. Turning, he collided with another passenger. "Sorry." He almost added "sir," but decided the bronze-faced man didn't look old enough. He twisted away from the man's hands roaming across his hoodie. *Watch it, Touchy.* The guy tugged at Nate's jacket once more before Nate glided past him and into the seat across from the boy and girl.

The pair had switched places. Now the boy sat in the aisle seat, and Hannah sat by the window with her gaze fixed forward.

"Hey," he croaked in her direction because he wanted someone to freak-out with. "What do you think is going on?"

Her gaze shifted to the ceiling, and she drummed her fingers rapidly against her thigh in a way that made him think she needed to pee. *What was up with that?*

"They're probably checking out a suspicious person," the boy with the earphones answered. It surprised Nate that the boy even heard the question. His music was loud enough to make out the tune even without the earphones. "It happens sometimes." The boy shrugged.

"Yeah, thanks," Nate said. Now that Hannah was ignoring him, he couldn't help studying her. Her warm cinnamon skin glowed against her fluffy pink blouse and made her look like sunrise. Her legs were hidden from view now, but he remembered how her pale-colored stockings matched her flat-heel shoes.

What kind of girl even dressed like that anymore? Everything about her flustered him. He swallowed, wishing his tongue hadn't swelled to the size of a Moray eel earlier so he could have at least mumbled 'Hello'.

After forty-five minutes, the plane was still in lockdown. When a security team finally arrived half an hour later, they asked everyone to show identification. Nate's only ID was his B-Prep student badge. Hannah and the boy had no ID at all.

"This violates our civil rights!" A passenger built like a bull shouted and stormed up the aisle from the rear. In seconds, two of the newly arrived G-men charged him and slammed him to the floor.

*Thanks, Mr. Bull; you've just guaranteed us all a longer delay.* The G-men hauled the guy to his feet then dumped him into a seat.

"You can't hold people without cause!" Mr. Bull spewed a string of four-letter words as his face turned bright red. Two more G-men joined the uproar, and out the window, a dozen more government-types rushed the plane.

Nate glanced about and met the worried and scared gazes of other passengers. The one exception was the bronze-faced man who had bumped into him. The guy looked calm, like nothing unusual was happening.

"You kids are with me." Startled, Nate glanced up. A young agent with a serious face and a blond crew cut motioned him to stand. "I'll escort you to the terminal so your guardians can verify where you'll be staying."

*Fine by me*, Nate took the lead while the boy and Hannah followed with the agent bringing up the rear.

"Can you tell us what this is about?" the ear-phoned boy asked.

"National security," the agent said like it should be enough explanation. Their plane had landed at least 200 yards from the arrival gate. They marched across several runways strangely void of any other planes.

In the terminal, the agent jotted down his grandparents' license numbers and address before releasing him to their custody. The agent then walked off with Hannah and the boy in tow.

"They finally let you off the plane," Granddad said. "What happened to make them hold people for so long?"

"I don't know," Nate said. "They said something about national security."

"Well, we have you now," Grandma said. "And oh my goodness! Look how skinny you are."

"Grandma, look how tiny you are," he teased and patted the top of a silvery head that only reached his chest. He gave her bird-like frame a gentle hug then shook Granddad's hand.

"Would you be up for a game of chess, young man?" Granddad, though ancient, still stood as straight as ever and beat Nate's height by two inches. Nate smiled at the challenge.

"I've gotten better," he warned.

"Well, you would have to." Granddad's mouth puckered as he tried to stifle a laugh.

"All right, it is *on*," Nate threatened and grinned. Seeing his grandparents again almost made him forget the miserable summer ahead.

They found the elevator to baggage claim. Before stepping inside, he spotted Hannah and the boy. So many people were hugging them; it looked like a family reunion happening at the airport.

Maybe the feel of his gaze caused Hannah to look his way. He met her eyes and waved, a little one, in case she ignored him again, but she waved back. Next, he smiled and got one in return. *Yes!* He resisted the urge to jump into the air and give her two thumbs up like a dork, but he still grinned like one. He wished he had the nerve to walk over and ask for her number so this summer wouldn't suck so much.

He noticed another passenger checking her out, but then realized she just stood in the man's line of sight. The guy, whom Nate recognized as Bronze-Face from the plane, looked past her and focused on his grandparents and him.

The man appeared again as Granddad pulled the car out of short-term parking. Apparently, Mr. Bronze-Face wasn't in any hurry to get to his own car or find a cab because he kept standing there, watching as they drove away.

# 3
# THE FARM

"Y ou're growing like a weed," Grandma said from the front passenger seat of the silver-gray Lincoln.

"I guess I didn't get your genes, Grandma." He'd sprouted four inches since his grandparents' Thanksgiving visit and had already heard the same comment from every grown-up he knew.

His grandparents proceeded to name all the men in the family who had inherited the tall gene while Nate took in the North Carolina countryside.

Under a brilliant blue sky, colorful wild flowers grew along the sides of the highway. The Smoky Mountains were visible in the distance and surrounding their peaks loomed the dense haze of fog that gave the mountains their name. Still, just because North Carolina looked like a post card, didn't mean he wanted to be there.

"You don't want to confuse your grandparents with gadgets," Mom had said when he asked to bring some type of handheld for the summer. The truth was that Grandma and Granddad didn't mind technology, as long as they didn't have to learn to use it. This attitude of theirs was weird, considering they had both been college professors.

He sighed. Only fifteen minutes into the summer and already he was bored. The farther they drove, the fewer cars they passed. An occasional house sprouted along the high cliff, and miles passed without any buildings except for an occasional mom and pop gas station.

The radio tortured him with an hour of gospel music before the car pulled off the highway. They drove through a rusty iron gate where tangled shrubs and vines wrestled along the side of a red-dirt road. After five minutes, the bumpy road forked. One trail ran into the woods while the other half met a paved brick driveway that led to a house about a mile away. A well-kept lawn circled the house for about an acre before transforming into wild green meadows.

Granddad parked near the house's front entrance. Nate followed his grandparents out of the car, baffled by the surroundings. He had imagined the farm as a small place on an acre or two of land with a barn and some animals. Instead, the farm consisted of a stately three-story white-framed house with six gigantic columns standing like sentries around the wrap-a-round porch. Rows of ancient look- ing magnolias bordered both sides of the driveway, and wild flowers of every hue covered the sloping hills like a rainbow on the ground. There wasn't a barn, or a tractor, or even a haystack in sight.

"This is the farm?" he asked his grandparents, already standing at the rear of the Lincoln.

"Well, it's not really a farm anymore." Grandma chuckled at the expression on his face and patted his cheek. "But it once was. We've gotten so used to calling this place a farm."

"Oh." Nate pulled his gaze away from the house. "What kind of farm?"

"Mostly tobacco. I think they tried to grow cotton once upon a time, but the weather was too cold for a good yield," Granddad an- swered and opened the trunk.

"Well, I guess it's a good thing you're not growing tobacco any- more," Nate said. "They lecture us in school about the danger of smoking and stuff."

"Yes, I know," Granddad said, "but times were different then. We didn't know then what we know today."

"So when did this place stop being a farm?" he asked.

"Well, let's see." A sly smile played upon Granddad's lips. "I took over the farm from my father in 1955, and by 1960 I had run the place completely into the ground."

Grandma shook her head and told Granddad to shoo. "Don't listen to him, Nathan," she said. "He did inherit the farm, but we decided to pursue teaching careers. Neither of us had a heart for farming." She waved her arm toward the rolling land with nostalgic yearning in her eyes. "Our choices were to put our heads in books or our hands in soil. On a place this big, we couldn't do both. We chose books. As the years passed, the fields grew into lawn and meadows, but we've never stopped calling this place a farm."

"So, how did our family come to own this place?" he asked.

The question seemed to stick in the air. His grandparents were quiet, and a look passed between them like they had a secret they did not want to share.

"We can talk about that later." Granddad pulled the larger of two bags from the trunk and headed for the house with Grandma at his side.

Nate grabbed the smaller bag, closed the trunk, and lagged behind. Had it been his imagination or had his grandparents avoided answering a question? His question was a fair one. An African-American family running a huge tobacco farm in the South couldn't have been ordinary, especially in the early part of the last century. From what he read in history books, there was a time when Blacks couldn't own land at all in the South. Yet, his family had owned this impressive piece of land for generations. How many generations, and what was it that Granddad and Grandma didn't want to talk about?

# 4
# HIDDEN

Grandma and Granddad reached the house ahead of him and looked down from the high porch as he approached the first step.

"Do you need any help, dear?" Grandma teased.

"I didn't know we were in a race, Grandma. Warn me next time." He climbed the steps two at a time to the top.

Wicker patio furniture filled the center of the porch, and a pair of playground swings hung from the clapboard ceiling. He wondered if his mom had once played on them. Then again, maybe the swings were one of the ways his grandparents passed the time. The mental image of them playing on the swings like kids made him smile, and he regretted thinking them capable of keeping secrets a few moments earlier.

"I hope you don't mind, Nathan." Granddad opened the door they apparently kept unlocked. "You'll be alone on the second floor. I'm afraid your grandma doesn't do stairs the way she used to. We have a room off the kitchen." He nodded in the direction Nate guessed must be the kitchen.

"Nah, that's cool."

"Good, I'll show you up." Granddad lugged the heavy suitcase toward the stairs. "We'll give you a tour of the place after lunch. Do we have a deal?"

"Yeah, it's a deal," Nate agreed. He trailed his granddad to the second floor where the hallway branched left and right. Granddad took the hallway leading right and came to a stop at the end of the corridor.

"We considered putting you in your mother's old room." Granddad nodded to a door directly across from them and then smiled as if he'd said something funny. "But I think you will prefer this one." He opened the door to what would be Nate's room for the next two months. "Now, I need to help your grandma with lunch," he said, switching on the light. "Put your things away and come down when you finish."

Granddad went up the hall, and Nate stepped into a room twice as big as his bedroom back home. A bunch of toy biplanes hung from strings attached to an overhead chandelier, a modeled solar system rotated slowly above a corner desk, built-in bookcases flanked both sides of a fireplace, and sculpted dinosaurs bearing tiny fierce teeth covered the mantel. It all looked old; maybe the room had been Granddad's when he was a kid. His grandparents must have figured he would like the room, and he would, if he were eight. *Seriously, did a Wii system never occur to them?* He shoved his bags into the closet to unpack later.

Out in the hallway, he eyed the door to his mom's old room and wondered why Granddad had thought making him stay there was funny. He walked over for a peek inside and found walls painted shocking pink with bright lavender trim around the crown molding and the window frames. With a white-ruffled comforter and lacy pillows smothering a wrought-iron bed, the room was sweet enough to cause tooth decay. Now he got his granddad's whacked humor and grinned.

The room's far wall had two more doors. One door led to the bathroom decorated in the same pink overkill. Next to the bath, a walk-in closet had wood storage shelves stacked high with different sized boxes. Below the shelves were rods still jammed with clothes. But the closet and the bath, separated by a wall, should have been the same dimension. Yet the closet was shorter than the bathroom by at least five feet. Right-a-way he wondered if the house had a secret passage or a hidden compartment like in old houses on TV.

He studied the closet's back wall for some hint of a door in the rustic wood paneling, but no outline showed. Pushing against the wall didn't help either.

Unlike the rest of the room, the closet's walls were not plastered but lined with a kind of wood called knotty pine. He'd helped Dad build a potting stand for Mother Day last year from the same kind of wood. They had carved a slit into one of the natural dents inside a knot to use for hiding a spare house key.

He probed a finger into several knotholes, not actually expecting to find anything. After only a few holes, his finger found cool metal. Something *was* wedged inside the knot. He tried prying it up, thinking he found a key. It didn't budge so he pressed down and heard a click. The wall cracked.

He stepped back, congratulating himself for having the insight of a genius but jumped when the door slammed open against the wall then banged shut. The door crept open again in a way that seemed unnatural. A sudden flow of hot air rushed past with the smell of mold and old lumber. A reversed suction must have pulled out the waves of dust particles that floated around him.

He stared mystified at the strange happening until an inhalation of dusty air made him sneeze three times and snapped him out of the daze. He waved away dust particles to no effect then stepped through the threshold and found a switch.

Amber light instantly poured from a single overhead bulb above a steep, narrow stairway. Strands of thick cobwebs dangled everywhere and dust caked every surface. Nate bounced on the balls of his feet to test the platform's sturdiness. The staircase groaned and squeaked at the unaccustomed movement, like it didn't appreciate being disturbed. Complaining stairs would not stop him from finding out where they led, but it cautioned his steps as he headed down.

The first ten or so steps ended at a halfway point on a small landing. The steps made a ninety-degree turn then continued into deeper shadows. He followed them down until he reached a dim alcove about four feet wide from side-to-side. A dead end as far as he could tell, but a door had to be hidden in the walls and probably opened with a buried latch like the closet overhead.

He hadn't thought to check for another light switch on the middle landing, even though a lot of the amber light had been lost with the stair's ninety-degree turn. He decided to backtrack and look for a middle switch, but he stopped when a shadow moved along the wall above him. For a moment, the long slender silhouette blocked any light from reaching the alcove. Then the shadow moved, releasing the light as it traveled farther down. Fear filled his chest as he shifted to flight mode.

Out of nowhere, a burst of frigid wind shot past him as if someone had let in a blast of arctic air. The cold chilled him to the bone as it swept up the stairs. Grumbling from the stairs came along with the sound of footsteps racing to the top. At least it sounded like footsteps, and yet, no one was on the stairs.

Something bumped him from behind. He jumped. Whirling around, he realized he'd moved backward without thinking and had collided with the wall. He almost laughed with relief but immediately tensed again. More squeaks and cracks came from above and were getting closer.

"Granddad?" He swallowed to take the edge out of his voice. "Grandma?" No answer. Still, something was nearly on him. He was trapped.

# 5
# SECRETS

The shadow reappeared and moved slowly along the wall then vanished into the dark of the landing. It lurked there. Pausing. Using the gloom like a cloak.

He told himself this was crazy thinking. Maybe only a band of scurrying rats moving from floor to ceiling. *Yeah, maybe.* Except light wouldn't stretch the shadows of rats so much. *Not even a gang of rats.*

More likely, a draft had found its way into the old passage, making the dangling overhead light bulb sway and causing shadows to seem as though they moved. He let the thought loop around his head a few times and refused to consider how this didn't explain the creaking still coming from the stairs. He had to face whatever was coming or cower in one of the alcove's poor excuse of a corner.

He took a step forward but before his foot reached the first incline, something shoved at his chest. He went flying backward. **Thud-plunk** into the wall, landing in a sprawl and hitting his head on the plank floor. Muffled clinking noises rattled from somewhere. The impact must have jiggled loose the hidden latch because the wall behind him shifted open.

Warm light flooded the small alcove and the icy chill vanished like it was never there. Nate scrambled to his feet and glanced about for an intruder but found no one and saw nothing to account for his fall. Only silence from the stairs now, but he had not imagined the cracks and squeaks before. Freaky.

He took a deep breath and tugged at his hoodie. He stepped from the tiny alcove into an airy sunlit room where a pair of sheer white curtains stirred lazily on a breeze from an open window. In front of the window, a small round table was set with a service for three.

"Nathan?" Grandma said in surprise as he emerged through the door.

"Grandma!" He supposed a secret passage ending in the kitchen was as good a destination as any, but ... "Why is there a secret stairway?"

"Oh, it's not secret, dear," Grandma said in a soothing tone, "it's concealed."

He paused to consider the difference between 'secret versus concealed' and decided there wasn't any. He was considering how to point this out to Grandma when Granddad entered the room.

"I see you found the back stairs, Nathan. Doing some exploring, eh? Close that cupboard, would you?"

*Cupboard?* Nate looked back the way he came. A china cupboard with glass doors, swayed from three hinges. The cupboard squeaked as he swung it back into place then settled into the wall with a soft click. *Oh, yeah, secret.*

He was relieved to see his granddad, maybe now he could get some answers.

"Granddad, why is the back stairway concealed?" he asked, deliberately using Grandma's word.

His grandparents exchanged another 'don't tell Nathan the secret' look.

"Well, it's mostly a matter of aesthetic. They may have once had a service, but they're not very attractive. We prefer they blend in with the wall."

If this weren't his granddad, Nate would ask if he was kidding. If it's only about the way it looks, why do the stairs end inside a bedroom closet?

"You must be tired from your long trip," Grandma said. "Lunch is almost ready. Why don't you wash up?"

"Yeah, okay." His grandparents obviously didn't want to talk about whatever they didn't want to talk about. "Do you have a downstairs bathroom I can use?"

"Yes, but why don't you just clean your hands at the sink, dear."

He washed at the kitchen's oversized white porcelain sink then dried his hands on a dishtowel. He turned to his grandma. "Mom always makes me do something to help with meals."

"No offense." Grandma blew a kiss and patted his cheek. "But you would only be in the way. We have a routine. Now, go wait at the table and rest."

His grandparents stood shoulder-to-shoulder at a counter in the large kitchen and worked as if they could read each other's minds. The scent of fresh bread drifted from the oven and a breeze from the opened window tickled his skin. Grandma and Granddad asked questions about school, friends, and his new interests. He suspected they wanted to keep his mind off the stairway. Still, he wondered how many other secret passageways this house had.

*Hold up!* The table rattled as his knee jerked against it. *Mom knows!* "Can I use the phone to call Mom?" he asked. "Oh, and Dad too," he added quickly.

Of course, dear," Grandma said. "The phone is behind you."

He turned. Did she mean the long black box hanging on the wall? It had a bell-like mouthpiece and a similar looking earpiece on a stretch of cord. *Was that a rotary dial?* This had to be an Alexander Graham Bell original.

"Grandma, what do you get when you cross a telephone with a pair of pants?" he asked.

"I'm afraid I don't know, dear."

"Bellbottoms," he told her. Grandma chuckled, but Granddad shook his head and moaned.

"I didn't think you kids knew about bellbottoms," Grandma said. "They're from your mother's days."

"Oh, I thought they wore petticoats and corsets," Nate teased. Now Grandma moaned.

"I think you should make your call before you dig yourself into a hole," Granddad said.

But the phone's nerd appeal wasn't the only reason he didn't want to call within his grandparents' hearing. *A little privacy would be nice.* "So, Grandma, is this your only phone?"

"No, we have one of those push-button phones in the music room off the foyer."

"Oh yeah? Do you think I could use that one? I'm... well, better at push buttons."

"Certainly, that phone is on the same line as this one. Your grandfather and I can talk to her from here when you call."

"Yeah, great," he said, "but I want to talk to her alone a minute first. Is that okay?"

"Of course it's okay, dear. Take as much time as you need. Just remember to let us say hello before you hang-up."

"Thanks." He stood, but didn't know which of two opened doors in the kitchen led to the foyer.

"That one, Nathan." Granddad pointed with the knife he was using to slice a melon. "Go through the door next to the refrigerator."

Nate reached the foyer, painted apple red with black marbled floors and dark molding. The massive space had a width of at least forty feet and was equally long. Two mahogany high-back benches with matching entrance tables furnished the oversized space. Fancy gold frames, with portraits of people he supposed were by-gone relatives, hung along the wall. At the bottom of each framed picture, a small copper plaque was engraved with the name, birth date, and the date of death of the person in the photo.

Catching a glimspe of a name beneath one photo, he stopped to study the picture. According to the copper plaque, this had been Nathan Freedman IV. He walked along the row of portraits until he found Nathan Freedman III, a Jr., and one Nathan Freedman without a suffix.

With Freedman as his middle name, Nate was named after his granddad. Granddad had been named for his father, but now he realized the name went back even further. The Nathan Freedman without the suffix died in 1863, which he was pretty sure, was the same year as the Emancipation Proclamation.

The man staring at him from the frame had a nose like his, but a leanness that made him look haunted, or maybe just sad. Had this Nathan Freedman been a slave? He took in the large foyer and wondered how a slave had owned a place like this.

The past surrounding this house posed lots of questions that needed answers. He hoped his mom wouldn't be as closed mouth on the subject as his grandparents. He found the music room then flopped into a chair beside the phone and dialed home.

# 6
# THE BONE

Mom picked up on the first ring as if she had been waiting for the call.

"Nathan, well finally! How long have you been there?"

He checked his watch. "About three hours."

"Three hours?" she repeated, sounding peeved. "And you're just getting around to calling?"

"Mom, the airport is over an hour away, and I had to unpack," he said like he hadn't only shoved his suitcases into the closet. "This is the first chance I've had to call." He'd forgotten his promise to phone home when he arrived. Stuff like a hidden passageway had distracted him.

"All right," Mom said. "How did your flight go? Did you have any problems?"

Telling her about the delay on the tarmac would steer her away from what he wanted to talk about. "Nope. No problems."

"Did you have any trouble finding your grandparents at the airport?"

"No, they were waiting for me."

"Good. I miss you, sweetheart." Her voice went mushy and he smiled.

"Mom, I've been gone for all of five hours. I'm away in school longer."

"Yes, but you've never been so far from home without us. I miss you. How's everything going?"

This was his cue. "Mom," he said, "why didn't you ever tell me about this place? How did our family come to own it?"

25

"Oh... well... honey, our family used to farm. I guess we still think of it that way."

Her tone told him she knew that wasn't what he meant. Mom didn't want to give out answers either. What was up here? Why send him to a place where they knew he would ask questions and then not answer the questions?

"Mom," he tried again, "Did something happen here that I should know about? Cuz' I'm starting to think there is."

"Nathan," her voice shifted from mushy to firm, "you're letting your imagination get the best of you. You're not there to ask questions and upset your grandparents. You are to use your stay to get a feel for our history and the people you come from. You have a proud heritage and you need to start acting accordingly. Reading a family secret into something so simple is really an overactive imagination."

"Really, Mom?" he said, "I'm supposed to be so awed by my ex-slave ancestor starting this farm that I change the way I act? Just like that?" What made them think he had a lack of pride anyway? The plan was lame. Then he thought about the walls full of noble-looking ancestors, staring down with piercing brown eyes and seeming to demand that you make an account of yourself. Okay, maybe the plan would work on someone who needed an attitude adjustment, but his did not.

*Dang, she's good!* He shook his head at his mom's nearly successful attempt at distraction. She and his grandparents *were* hiding something.

"What about the secret staircase?" he asked. Her silence told him he had caught her off guard. "Mom?" he said. "Did you hear me?"

"Um, yes, honey. You found the back stairs?"

"Yeah, wasn't too hard."

"Well okay, yes, the house may have a history," she admitted, "but we're not going to discuss it over the phone."

Nate stood from the chair, wishing he wasn't tied to the spot by the outdated phone. "Well, why won't Grandma and Granddad talk about it? They act weird every time I bring it up."

"Nathan, we will not continue this discussion. Now you mind what you are told and stop bothering people about it. Do you understand me, little boy?"

*Little boy?* That's what she called him when she meant to imply he was acting immature.

Frustrated, he shoved a hand into a pocket of his hoodie and knuckled something he didn't remember putting there. Absently, he rubbed a finger across the slim, smooth surface as he paced in front of the chair.

"Mom, in three years I'll be old enough to fight in a war. So don't treat me like a child."

"First, you'll be fighting in wars over my dead body. And second, you shouldn't force people to discuss something they find painful. So show a little consideration for other people's feelings. Are we clear?"

He didn't answer. He rotated the thing in his pocket and wondered what horrible act had happened here to make his family so secretive.

"Your father wants to speak with you." Her voice sounded misty again. "I love you, sweetheart. Call home soon."

He sank into the chair as he waited for his father to take the line. He pulled the found object from his pocket and frowned at a USB.

"Nate?" Dad's deep voice boomed from the receiver.

"Hey, Dad."

"Sounds like you found yourself a bone, son."

"Yeah, I guess."

"Well, you know what dogs do with bones don't you?"

"They bury them?"

"Yeah, some do, and some never let go."

His spirit soared. Mom had shut him down; but was Dad giving him a green light?

"Nate?" his father's voice came again.

"Yeah, Dad?"

"What kind of dog are you?"

"O-kaay," he said slowly. "Where's Mom?" Dad would never openly contradict her.

"She's in the kitchen crying," he said. "Nate, this thing has gnawed at the family long enough. See if you can uncover the truth while you're down there."

"I'm on it, Dad." For a moment, Nate wondered if this had been Dad's ulterior motive from the start. "Can you give me a hint about what I'm suppose to find the truth to?"

"Just dig for the facts, then form your own conclusion."

"Yes, sir."

"Take care not to upset your grandparents now."

"I won't."

"Good. Your mom wants to speak with her folks. I'll get her; you get them on the line."

"Thanks, Dad."

"Love you, son."

Nate started for the kitchen then realized he forgot to mention the USB. It must belong to Dad. He set it against the phone to remind himself to ask about it the next time they talked. He walked to the kitchen and told Grandma his mom was on the line, then returned to the music room and placed the receiver into the cradle. The black USB had all but disappeared against the black phone. He considered moving it so he wouldn't forget about it, but nowhere else looked any better so he let it stay.

Walking across the foyer, he paused again at the portraits. His granddad never used the suffix, but Nate guessed that in the line of Freedmans, Granddad must be the fifth. Granddad only had a sister. Already on the wall, she had died childless. His parents wanted another child, but couldn't have one after him. That made him the last of the Freedman's bloodline, but he didn't intend for things to stay that way. He wanted children someday.

He doubted his grandparents had skeletons hidden in their closet. They were just too good. Whatever shamed the Freedman's name must have happened even before their time, unless it had something to do with his mom. He could see Mom raising all kinds of trouble. Except Dad had encouraged him to find the truth, and he wouldn't if Mom had anything to hide. No, uncovering the truth probably meant searching the house's past.

He turned toward the kitchen again and shivered from a sudden chill. His mom would say that kind of chill meant someone was walking across your grave. That never made sense to him. How could someone walking across your grave bother you when you didn't even have a grave yet? This pondering died as a blast of cold air blew into the room, whipping out of nowhere. He shielded his face at the flurry of wind gusts. It lasted a few seconds then the air grew unnaturally still. He squinted at a frame tilted on the wall. *What the…*

Weird. The picture of Nathan Freedman the First was now hanging upside down.

# 7
# THE PHANTOM SHADOW

"Nathan?" Granddad peered down at him. "Are you awake?" Nate checked the clock on the nightstand. *Eight-thirty.* "I don't think so, Granddad." He rolled over. "Can I sleep a little longer?"

"No, church is this morning."

"What time is church?" He pulled the sheet over his head. "It doesn't start 'til eleven back home."

"Be that as it may, your grandma has a Sunday school class to teach at ten, and we have a thirty-five-minute drive."

Nate stifled a moan. Church plus Sunday school guaranteed a mind-numbing day.

"Sorry to rush you." Granddad turned and walked to the door. "But you need to get moving if you want breakfast before we leave."

Granddad's footsteps echoed down the hall as Nate wondered about the odds of talking Granddad and Grandma into letting him skip church. He could better spend the time figuring out what needed investigating and looking into what his grandparents told him about Nathan Freedman's up-side-down picture. He lingered in bed and ran a hand over his head, remembering.

Yesterday, he had rushed to the kitchen and hauled his grandparents to the foyer to show them the topsy-turvy picture, but the photograph had righted itself by the time he returned.

"But ..." Baffled, he had pointed at the lying, deceitful picture hanging perfectly on the wall. "A minute ago it was messed up. All crooked and stuff."

"Hmmm, yes, we believe you, Nathan," Granddad said. "That picture turns upside down all the time."

"What?"

"Yes, dear. We're sorry if it scared you," Grandma had added. "Months, even years go by without an incident, but every now and again something appears to want attention."

Nate had turned with an an open-mouth stare at them. "You're serious? You mean a ghost turned the picture?"

"Of course." Grandma had surveyed Nathan Freedman's portrait thoughtfully. "Your mom believes something is holding him here."

Nate had blinked a couple of times, and then managed to ask calmly, "Does everyone in this family believe in ghosts?"

"Well, what would you call it, dear?" Grandma asked.

*Weird*, Nate thought again. He unfolded from the covers, stretched, and swung his legs out of bed. Without a plan of action, he had to face the torture of church.

In the bathroom, a pedestal sink sported separate spigots for hot and cold water, and a claw-foot tub took the place of a shower. He knelt in the tub and did his best to bathe without the convenience of a showerhead. Cascades of water ran over his knees before reaching the drain, but the soft gurgles didn't muffle a floorboard cracking beyond the still open door of the bathroom. A louder crack followed by a squeak made him turn off the water to listen. An uneasy stillness made it seem as though someone listened back. A faint squeak came again. He wrapped a towel around his waist and left wet footprints as he padded across the black and white tiled floor. From behind the bathroom door, he poked his head into the room as the last of a blurry shadow ducked into the hallway, or at least, he thought it had been a shadow. Even stranger, the room now smelled like some kind of incense or spice.

"Granddad? I'm almost ready," Nate called, but received no reply. Still, to avoid keeping his grandparents waiting, he went to the walk-in closet to dress.

The closet was more than half the size of his entire bedroom back home and even had a window. This vantage point gave him a clear view of Granddad on the driveway below, busy cleaning the windshield of the Lincoln. Thoughts of ghosts must have him imagining things. If Granddad was washing the windshield, then no way had he been in the hallway a minute ago. Maybe this house did have a ghost, but that didn't explain the shadow. How would a ghost have a shadow? And what about the incense smell? *A ghost's odor?*

He pushed ideas of restless spirits away and concentrated on getting dressed. Mom had packed a suit jacket for the trip. Good thing since his favorite hoodie had collected dust and cobwebs during his exploration of the attic yesterday after lunch. "No air conditioning up there." Granddad had warned. *No kidding.* It had been like a walk through a furnace. He took off the hoodie in the attic, but not before it collected enough grime to need cleaning.

He knelt on the floor of his closet and frowned when he opened the suitcase he still hadn't unpacked. Someone had pulled out his neatly folded clothes and shoved them carelessly back in again. His suit jacket, along with everything else, was crammed into a wrinkled mess.

*Great!* The airline kept them on the tarmac for almost two hours. Enough time for agents to search through their stuff. He pulled out the wrinkled jacket and hung it on one of the hooks mounted along the wall. Maybe his hoodie would be okay with a good dusting off. He walked into the bedroom to get it but the hoodie was missing from the desk chair where he dropped it after coming down from the attic. He searched the room but with no luck. He only hoped his grandparents were not as offended by wrinkled clothes as his mom.

A breakfast of pancakes dripping with butter and maple syrup waited for him on the kitchen table. Grandma and Granddad had sworn off meat a few years back, but the soy sausage links tasted almost as good as the real thing. He gulped up the fake meat and washed it down with a large glass of orange juice.

"Grandma," he said through a mouthful of pancakes, "why did tofu cross the road?"

Grandma shot him a doubtful look. "Why, dear?"

"To prove he wasn't a chicken."

She shook her head and smiled. "You only have a few minutes to eat. Finish up."

He grinned and devoured the rest of the pancakes in a few bites. Minutes later, they settled into the car for the drive to church. He marveled again at the scale of the house. When the blinds at a corner window parted slightly, the hairs of his neck prickled. Was someone peering out from inside the house?

Granddad perfected a three-point turn, and then drove down the driveway. Nate kept his gaze on the house, watching for more movement at the window as the car neared a bend.

Peeping from behind blinds didn't seem very ghost-like. A ghost could stand on the front porch to watch them leave and still be unseen, right? For a moment, he considered the possibility of a drifter secretly living in his grandparent's house. Maybe the drifter occasionally turned pictures upside down to make Granddad and Grandma believe in ghosts and discount unexplained noises. Maybe the drifter wore spicy cologne. Of course, that theory only made sense if a drifter had been living in the house for years because his mom knew about it and she had left home ages ago. Still, something definitely odd was happening inside his grandparents' house.

Granddad drove the car around the bend, putting the house completely out of sight, and Nate turned his attention to a more immediate concern.

# 8
# AN ALLY

Nate made mental notes on the directions to town. He planned to bike to town using one of the bicycles he found in the attic yesterday and do research on the library's computers. By the time they reached the town of Victory, he'd scratched the biking idea. It took his speed-demon granddad twenty-five minutes to reach the town. Nate estimated at least a three-hour round trip by bike, and that was allowing for only one hour of research. He needed a more doable plan.

After another ten minutes, they pulled off the main road and drove up a hill to a small, white church with a tall steeple. Granddad parked in the graveled lot under an old oak. Nate followed his grandparents inside the church with all the enthusiasm of a convicted criminal walking to the guillotine.

Grandma prepared her Sunday school class in the church's combination recreation/dinning area, while Nate tagged behind Granddad to the front pews where a group of men had gathered. Granddad introduced them as the church deacons. After a few minutes of their company, Nate decided few things were more boring than old men talking about the weather.

Mercifully, more parishioners arrived. He scanned for kids his age, but this town's population of high school kids had done a better job of dodging church than he. Most of the kids looked like boring middle schoolers.

Grandma waved from the entrance. He waved back but silently groaned when she started over. He hoped she didn't intend to make him sit with the little kids in her class.

"Nathan." Grandma reached him and took his hand. "Come, dear." She led him out the sanctuary to the recreation area. A teenage girl stood in the center of the room, trying to control about a dozen little kids running about.

"Now what are the odds?" Grandma said as they approached the girl whose shoulder-length hair fell across her face as she peered at a boy tugging her skirt.

"Remember the girl and boy with you when that nice young agent brought you to us at the airport?" Grandma continued. "Well, they turned out to be my best friend's grandchildren! They're down for a visit too." They approached the girl, and Grandma tapped her shoulder to get her attention. Heat rushed to his face as the girl straightened and faced them.

"Dear, this is Nathan. You recall seeing him on the plane, don't you?"

"Nathan," Hannah said as his heart pounded wildly against his chest. "What a nice name." She offered her hand and another one of her dazzling smiles.

"Yeah, hey." He couldn't believe his good luck. The girl from the plane was in his grandparents' church. Things were looking up.

"Nathan, Hannah," Grandma said. "You can both be a big help today. Why don't you each take three of these little ones, and we can teach in small groups."

His mind plummeted from the cloud it had been drifting on and hit concrete. Had Grandma suggested *he* teach Sunday school? She had a ton of faith if she believed he rolled like that.

Hannah wasted no time collecting three of the children closest to her and then led them to a kid-size table. She pulled a Bible from her purse and gave the children a radiant smile.

Nate recovered from the grandma-induced shock and said, "I wish I could, Grandma, but I can't."

Grandma walked around the room and collected three boys. "You'll have fun. You'll see. Just don't tell them any jokes." She guided the boys toward him. "Here you go, dear."

"But I *really* can't," he pleaded.

"You'll be fine." She flicked her hand like she wanted him to get on with it and then gathered up the remaining children to begin her Sunday school class.

Nate stood in the middle of the room without a clue to his next move. He spotted a quiet corner and walked over. He dropped to the floor and scooted into the corner as far as the wall allowed. All three boys followed quietly and sat on the floor beside him, taking the same crossed leg position. Then came the questions.

"What's your name?" one asked.

"Where're you from?" said another.

Nate glanced longingly at the door, still searching for an excuse to leave. Grandma seemed to read his mind because she looked over and nodded in that way people do when they're trying to be encouraging.

He blew out a breath of despair. He wondered how Hannah managed to keep so cool.

"Is Miz Ultima your mama?" More questions from a boy pointing to Grandma. "Is she your girlfriend?" The same boy pointed to Hannah.

Nate looked at the three wide-eyed question monsters for the first time. They were about six or seven and didn't seem too bratty.

"Nah, chill okay? Mrs. Ultima is my grandma, and I don't have a girlfriend. Now, that's enough questions from you guys. It's my turn to ask the questions, all right?"

"Okay," they said in unison. "What kinda questions?" one asked.

Nate grinned; they were sort of fun. "That's a question," he said. "My turn, remember?"

"Okay," said the three in unison once more and then burst into giggles.

"Good," said Nate, "first, what do I call you?"

****

They were still talking in the corner forty minutes later when Grandma interrupted.

"Nathan, Sunday school is over. The boys' parents are waiting."

"Sorry, Grandma." He stood. "Later, little bros."

"Nate, come meet my mama." The boy grabbed his hand.

"All right," Nate said and was tugged over to a group of people standing near the door.

When he rejoined his grandma, she was talking with Granddad, Hannah, and three people he didn't know.

"Nathan," Grandma said, "say hello to our best friends, Mabel and Henry Green, Hannah's grandparents."

Nate stuck out his hand, which Hannah's grandfather shook and her grandmother squeezed. "Nice to meet you," he said.

"And this." Grandma beamed up at a man with short dreadlocks as if he was a favorite son. "This is Reverend Ellis."

"Nathan," Reverend Ellis said, "your grandparents talk about you all the time." He shook Nate's hand and patted his shoulder. "Good to finally meet you."

"Church won't start for another few minutes," Grandma said. "Why don't you and Hannah get some fresh air while we grown-ups talk?"

"Yeah, okay." He turned to Hannah. "You want to take a break?" he asked. Hannah nodded.

Outside, he scanned the parking area for a place to sit. "How about my grandparents' car?" He pointed to the Lincoln under the oak tree, and Hannah nodded again.

He gave her his hand as she climbed onto the hood. He glided onto the car with a fluid movement and nervously ran his palms along the seams of his trousers.

"I'm glad I got the chance to see you again." His voice cracked as another surge of hormones threatened to erupt.

"Me too," she said and seemed as relaxed as he was tense.

"So, was that your brother on the plane with you? Where's he?" he asked, not because he cared, he just couldn't think of anything else to say.

"Oh, not much can make William come to church these days," she answered softly.

He wondered if she used everyone's proper name. *Really, what kind of girl did that?* "Yeah? Too bad," he said. "He might have liked it. I didn't want to come, but I'm glad I did." He ran a hand across his smooth head. "Now you." He nodded and gave her his best 'you bad' look. "You looked like you owned the church the way you handled those kids." He considered saying she must be an angel, but vetoed the line as lame.

Hannah smiled. "Well, church is a staple in my family. I can't recall a time when I didn't attend." She arched a brow like she was impressed. "You didn't do too badly. It seems as though you were a big hit with the boys. What did you teach them?"

"I don't know," he said. "We talked about the parallels between *Star Wars* and the Bible. You know, good, evil, and redemption."

Hannah's eyelashes went into a blinking spasm. "That's very unconventional."

"Yeah, I suppose." The statement sounded like a reprimand, but her shocked expression made him laugh despite his best effort to suppress it.

"All right." She softened and laughed too. "I can take things too seriously. I sound like a prude, right?"

"No, it's not that," he said. "You just remind me of someone else. She wouldn't have approved of my Sunday school lesson either."

"If the someone I remind you of is your mother, I shall be very upset with you."

"You shouldn't be," he said. "My mom is beautiful."

"Yes, I think she would have to be," Hannah said, openly assessing him.

His cheeks burned, and he glanced away to hide his embarrassment.

"And how is your visit going so far?" she asked.

"Interesting," Nate answered, trying to sound normal, but he could still hear the rush of blood in his ears.

"Interesting? That sounds interesting," she teased. "How so?"

"It's sort of hard to explain. There's something odd about the house that no one wants to talk about."

"Odd? How?"

"I'm not sure yet." The flush feeling she gave him passed, and he turned to her again. "Just something that upsets them."

Hannah's eyes lit up. "It sounds like a mystery."

"My father said I should solve it on my own, but I don't know where to start."

"Really? You're actually working on a mystery?" she asked but continued before he could answer. "Well, the first thing to do is surf the Internet. It's the world's vastest warehouse of information. But if this involves a crime, you should research back copies of old newspapers."

"'First off, the Internet is not an option. I've already thought about biking to the library to use a computer, but my grandparents' place is pretty isolated. They might wonder why I'm biking twenty-five miles to do research, and I'm not supposed to upset them."

"You and your grandparents don't have a computer?" Hannah questioned.

"I have a computer. But I couldn't bring it. I'm sort of being punished."

"Really? What on Earth did you do?" Again, she didn't wait for an answer. "I can help, if you want. I have my computer."

"Yeah? That would be awesome!"

"I'll let you know if I find anything. What's your cell number?"

He watched her take a notepad from her purse. Nate suspected she had a contingency plan for every situation inside her purse. He sure didn't walk around with bibles and notepads just in case the need arose.

"I could tell you my number, but my phone is back in Boston with my computer," he said. "I told you, punishment/life-lesson type thing going on here."

Hannah's lips pouted a little like she was disappointed, but then she said, "No problem, we'll come up with a communication plan after dinner."

He was lost. Did she just invite him for dinner? "What about dinner?" he asked.

"Your grandparents invited us. You didn't know?"

"No, but that'll be great." Just thinking about dinner with her brought heat to his face. "We should go back inside though." He slid off the hood then took Hannah's hand and helped her down. "Service should start soon."

Now that a hot girl was helping him, he didn't mind his parents' over-the-top punishment so much. Soon, they would find answers.

# 9
# ANSWERS

The doorbell chimed. "I got it." Nate stood from the table where he was shelling peas for dinner.

"Thank you, dear. The Greens are probably here." Grandma pulled a dish of blackberry cobbler from the oven. Nate's stomach growled from the sweet-tart smell filling up the kitchen. Granddad's stomach must have done some complaining too because Nate caught a glimpse of him heading over to the cobbler with a spoon as he darted out the door and hurried to the foyer.

He opened the door to Hannah and her grandparents, wondering if feeling goofy every time he saw her would last much longer. The feeling made him awkward when he wanted to be cool.

"Hey, come in," he greeted them. "Grandma and Granddad are in the back."

The Greens bustled into the house. They went straight to the kitchen and started helping as if they did it all the time. Nate stood with Hannah in the kitchen doorway, wondering if he should invite her to help finish shelling the peas or stay out of the way.

"Oh, yes, of course." Grandma paused, noticing them, but almost as if she'd forgotten they were there. "Why don't you show Hannah around, dear?"

"Okay, sure." He smiled. *Alone time with Hannah.* He checked his long stride to match her shorter steps as they headed to the foyer. "So, do you want a tour of the upstairs?" he asked when they entered the oversized hall.

"No, Nathan," she whispered. "Let's go sit down."

"Yeah, okay," he answered in the same hushed tone.

"Somewhere private," she added then turned and headed down the hall in the direction of the music room. Her heels clicked against the marble and echoed off the ceiling as she walked. Hannah reached the room and scanned it. Apparently deciding it was private enough, she entered.

Nate walked down the hall and stood on the threshold, wondering what she was up to until she waved him over.

"Hurry, Nathan, we don't have much time."

He hesitated because if she was thinking what he was thinking, then what was to stop one of their grandparents from walking in on them from the kitchen? Hannah moved fast for a girl. Wasn't *he* supposed to be the one making all the first moves? He walked to her slowly, with his heart thumping loud enough for her to hear. Hannah patted the spot beside her on the sofa.

"Nathan," she said, "start from the top."

"Oh, okay." He had no idea what she expected him to do. He didn't know how to start from the top. He didn't know anything.

"Nathan?" Hannah said, turning a quizzical face up to him.

"Yeah?"

"Tell me about your mystery."

"Oh yeah, right." He exhaled. "You want to hear about the mystery." He dropped into the seat beside her, relieved she didn't want to make out.

"Nathan, are you okay?"

"Sure." He swallowed and found his cool. "Well, something happened here."

"You mean the farm?" she asked.

"Yeah ... hey, wait," he said. "How do you know this was a farm?"

"I found something."

"You did? Already?"

"Oh, yes. This place is a local legend, but my grandparents did not care to talk about it either. I had to get whatever I could from the Internet, which was easier than I thought."

He frowned, "Hold up, your grandparents know something about this place?"

"Yes, I think most of the locals do."

"Well, what do they know?" He scooted to the edge of his seat.

"Nathan Freedman, not your grandfather but your great-great-great-great-great grandfather," Hannah said, counting off the number of greats on her fingers, "settled this place."

"Yeah, I think that's one great too many, but keep going." The excitement swelling in his chest was hard to control, but it seemed lost on Hannah. She turned to him with a look he couldn't read and then shook a finger at him.

"Now, simply because information is on the Internet doesn't mean it's true. So don't jump to any conclusions. Promise me, Nathan."

He immediately jumped to the conclusion that she did not have good news. Only bad news needed a warning. "Yeah, sure. I promise." He kept his foot from tapping the floor impatiently and smiled. "Soooo ..." He nodded, hoping to encourage her. "Go on."

"Okay. Nathan Freedman was born a slave, but earned enough money to buy his freedom. He moved to New York where his talent made him a sought-after builder." She looked at him. "I think it's nice the way your granddad is named for him."

"Yeah, he's not the only one." He gave her a rundown on the line of Freedmans hanging out on the foyer wall.

"Well, I don't wonder why. The man was a genius," Hannah said. "He understood architecture without ever having a formal education. His skills were in high demand. Some people believed he became rich. Then for some unknown reason, he moved to North Carolina at the height of his success. That's when he built this house." She looked around the room, appraisingly. "Nathan, this place is historic," she whispered and then drifted into silence like her mind had detoured to the house's antebellum past.

"Yeah," Nate said, nudging her back into the present. "We sort of know that."

Hannah smiled then continued. "A few years after he came here, North Carolina passed a proclamation prohibiting free Blacks from living in the state. The state gave your distant grandfather and others like him only three months to settle their affairs and leave. That's where all records of Nathan Freedman end. He just vanished," Hannah finished.

"Wow, you found all this on the Internet?"

"Well, a book about the lives of free Blacks during slavery has been scanned onto the Internet. Twenty-four prominent men have a biography written up in the book."

"And, Nathan Freedman is in this book?"

"Yes, it's very interesting." Something about the way her eyes drifted down bothered him.

He squinted. *What's she leaving out?* "What else did the book say about him?" he asked.

"Well," Hannah glanced up at the ceiling and twisted strands of her hair. "He became a farmer when he settled here."

"So he did farm?"

"Yes," Hannah said. "He built this house and started a farm."

"Yeah? That's good, right?" He still didn't understand why Hannah seemed uncomfortable. "So did the book say how he did it? I mean, being black and farming in the South during slavery?"

"The thing is …" Hannah's eyes fell to her lap then smoothed her skirt before continuing. "He's listed as a successful free man who owned slaves."

"What?" The breath went out of him as though a fastball hit him in the chest. *Slave owner?* He had always assumed he was a descendant of slaves, not slave owners. Now it seems his ancestors had been the oppressors, not the oppressed. Already, shame nibbled at his conscious. *Nathan Freedman had not been such a great man.*

"Nathan?" Hannah studied him with a worried face. "Remember, you promised not to jump to conclusions. Personally, I think we have too many unanswered questions to accept this account as true. We really do have a mystery."

"What do you mean?" He was still having trouble processing the information.

"For one thing." Hannah placed her hand over his. "Remember the proclamation? In 1830, he had to leave North Carolina and sell this house. However, that never happened. The house is still in your family. That's a mystery. And two, after North Carolina, why are there no records on him? He didn't return to his previous occupation because he built no houses afterward, at least according to the eBook. So there's another mystery."

"So? How would anybody even know if he built more houses or not?" Nate said. "Besides, he may have just died."

"His homes had a distinct signature. And ..." Hannah released his hand and gently tapped his forehead. "You're here, so he couldn't have died."

"What does that mean?" He rubbed his forehead even though the tap hadn't hurt.

"Nathan, no record of a marriage for Nathan Freeman exists. He would have had to register that information. Even that eBook lists him as single. But you exist, which proves he married and had a family, and it didn't happen until after 1830. So now we know he didn't die, we have to conclude he was in hiding."

"But why stay?" He looked at her suspiciously. *Was she joking?* "Are you sure he owned slaves?" he asked.

Hannah blinked slowly, like she was preparing to show more patience than she had. "I know this comes as a shock," she said, "but you need to get past the 'owned slaves' part and follow me. We have questions we need to ask. Why would an ex-slave who had bought his own freedom choose to come back and live in a state that condoned slavery? How did he manage to keep the house he built in your family after it became illegal for him to live here? And why—"

"I got it!" Nate snapped his finger as a crazy thought hit him with an awesome alternative to the messed-up version of his family's history. "I bet it's the reason for the secret stairway."

"A secret stairway?" Hannah said. "Nathan, this house has a secret passage?"

He nodded. "At least one, but probably more. Maybe Nathan Freedman used them to get around without anyone seeing him." He hoped the overactive imagination his mom accused him of having wasn't in play here. "You know what I think?"

Hannah nodded as if she really could read his mind. Excitement rushed her speech. "I do! I think it's very possible. One of the reasons North Carolina passed a proclamation was because they were convinced free Blacks were helping slaves escape."

He forced himself to rein in his mounting enthusiasm "So, we're thinking this house was a stop, right?"

Hannah's bright eyes flashed as she nodded repeatedly. Her grin stretched almost ear-to-ear. "Not a slave master." She beamed at him. "Nathan, he was a station master!"

"For the Underground Railroad," Nate said in a low voice. *Whew, so much better than slave owner!* "Why else would an ex-slave return to the South?"

"Right! And a plantation would be the perfect cover to hide freedom seekers," Hannah said.

"Okay, only," Nate said, "if he went into hiding after 1830, how did he operate the Railroad?"

"Good question. How did Harriet Tubman or Peg-Leg Joe do it? They used stealth, codes, and a network of supporters. Your distant grandfather would have needed help," Hannah said. "We don't think of white Southerners as sympathizers in the anti-slavery movement, but many were. I did a little research. Over six thousand North Carolinians left the state in protest of the proclamation. So continuing his mission would have been harder, but not impossible. At least one sympathizer had to help him."

"Hannah, from the time he couldn't own the land until the Emancipation Proclamation, was about thirty-five years. He spent all that time running the Railroad without anyone catching on. Seems like things might have been a little more complicated than help from a sympathizer can explain."

"My theory is the most reasonable explanation of events." She cocked a brow at him. "Unless you have a better one?"

"No, not yet."

"Then we'll go with mine."

He let it go. "So, somehow the truth got turned around and Nathan Freedman became a self-serving slaver?"

"I'm afraid so. People around here were pretty upset by it, too. The author got the story wrong. Before that book came out in 1964, the Freedman's name was revered."

"My family couldn't disprove any of this, so they've hushed-up about the house's history."

Hannah tilted her head as though considering something. "The thing about the Underground Railroad was its secrecy," she said. "Documenting activities was dangerous. The lack of documentation became the reason for the Railroad's success. If there were ever proof of an Underground Railroad connection to this house, it would have been hidden, well hidden. If you and I can find that link it would fix everything."

At that moment, he decided she *was* an angel— his angel. He swallowed a lump of gratitude building in his throat.

"What about his grave?" he said. "Shouldn't we think about finding it too? The date on the tombstone would prove he stayed."

Hannah squeezed his hand. "See, now we're back on the same page. I've already thought of that. Finding a black person's grave from that period is a huge task. Many were unmarked. Some were marked but with wood headstones that decayed long ago. Others were made of stone, but most have inscriptions worn away so badly the marking can no longer be read. We would need the best kind of luck."

He was about to respond when a weird sensation caused his voice to catch in his throat. Happiness flowed through him like rays of tranquil energy. The sensation came and passed as quickly as a stray breeze on a summer day. Yet it reminded him of the chilled air from the secret stairway and the gust of wind from the foyer. They all seemed to come suddenly and out of nowhere. If he believed the story his grandparents told, he would guess the house's ghost had just paid a visit.

An odd sensation hit him and he realized the ghost was smitten with Hannah. She was what made his frigid cold spirit-air go all warm and fuzzy.

Nate shook his head to rid himself of the weird sensation. He hoped Hannah hadn't noticed. "Yeah, I guess," he said, vaguely. The distraction from the ghost caused him to forget the last thing she said, so he leaned over and kissed her gently on the cheek. "Thanks."

Hannah smiled then lowered her head and looked so bashful, Nate couldn't resist a second kiss, but this time his lips fluttered hesitantly against hers until she moved her lips a hair closer, encouraging him, he hoped. He leaned in and wondered if she actually tasted like raspberries or if it was the taste of her lip-gloss. *Sweet!*

Their kiss lingered and turned into a third kiss, then a fourth, until he lost count. If not for the sound of footsteps on the foyer's marble floor, he might have kissed her all day.

# 10
# THE WOODS

Nate trudged through the wild undergrowth still thinking of Hannah and yesterday, before Granddad's terrible timing to announce dinner had ruined a perfect moment. Now, a daze drifted over Nate as he remembered Hannah's kiss.

A prickly limb slapped the side of his face, forcing his attention back to the rolling terrain. He paused and ran a hand across his cheek to check for blood. Seeing none, he pushed on through the woodsy landscape that was fast losing the appeal it held when viewed from the back porch.

His thoughts turned to Hannah again. She was the reason he was out stomping the woods. According to her, private cemeteries were common on large estates long ago. She proposed that Nathan Freedman's final resting place might lie somewhere on the property. After an hour of searching, he realized that even if she was right, the odds of finding the grave were slim. The old farm's acres of land made locating a cemetery a little like the needle in a haystack phrase his mom always used when trying to find anything in his room.

He weaved in and out of blackberry brambles and rows of fruit trees weighted down with plums, figs, or peaches. The orchard bordered a thick growth of wild woods. He sometimes strayed into the woods but never far enough to lose the gurgling sound of water running along the rock-covered brook below the orchards.

Grandma and Granddad had gone into town after breakfast for a meeting at the church and planned to shop for groceries afterward.

He wiggled out of the trip by pretending he wanted to read one of the classic books in his room. The excuse worked, his grandparents were all about reading. He had watched their car pull around the bend before going upstairs and dressing in clothes he hoped were right for hiking. Before leaving the house, he shoved two granola bars into the side pockets of his cargo pants and then left through the backdoor.

His goal was to survey the land for the most reasonable place to put a cemetery. That meant looking under every growth of vines thick enough to hide an old fence or broken headstones. For two hours, he found nothing more interesting than a pile of rocks. Then he came to a clearing where a gap in a mass of old trees resembled a yawning mouth.

Under maples, oaks, and evergreens, a carpet of leaves and fallen branches littered the ground. The leveled land looked like a good place for a cemetery, plus the canopies of trees kept the undergrowth low. He guessed a grave could easily be dug here. The grove went deep, with only a scattering amount of light occasionally filtering through the trees. Checking it out would take more time than he had. He was already pushing his luck and needed to head back to the farm to beat his grandparents home.

The day had grown hot, and a belly full of fruit from the orchards made walking back slower than the hike up. Inside his cargo pants, two plucked peaches knocked uncomfortably against his thigh.

He reached the edge of the hill and balanced himself, taking halting steps down until he came to the brook. The path was better worn here. Following the stream north, against the flow, he headed back to the farmhouse.

No longer focused on finding grave markers, he took in the breathtaking landscape and saw something he missed before. Sparks of sunlight glinted off something in the woods on the other side of the ravine.

Renewed excitement surged through him at the thought of the glint coming from a metal fence, like maybe a gate surrounding a cemetery. He hurried to cross the twenty-foot wide shallow stream dividing the land from the road.

His sneakers soaked up the chilled water as he waded into the brook with currents strong enough to tug his pants leg. Suddenly, one foot slid on a slippery rock that sent him crashing into the stream. Soaked.

He wiped gushing blood from a nasty cut on his palm against his shirt and then cupped the palm upright, hoping the blood would pool, clot, and seal the wound.

Standing in the stream, he avoided another fall by digging his feet into the rocky bed before each step. Slowly crossing the stream, he at last climbed onto the embankment where another obstacle, a deep slope, separated him from the dirt road below.

He treaded down the slope, and a few minutes later, stood on the dirt road. He guessed it to be the same one Granddad had taken through the rusty gate when they arrived from the airport. Using the road as his new compass, he walked along the shoulders, searching for another spark off something from the woods running alongside it.

He soon reached an industrial-sized, concrete pipe, sunk into a long gulley to bridge the road with the meadow. Some tall grass had flattened under muddy tire tracks that disappeared into the trees.

He followed the tracks into the cool shade of an ancient looking forest where the temperature dropped at least ten degrees. Under thick foliage, the calls of birds and the chattering of squirrels and chipmunks seemed magnified, as though their sound could not escape the green roof. The musty smell of decaying leaves and damp earth gave the place a primordial feel. His footsteps made hardly a sound on a ground cushioned by damp pine needles.

So fascinated by the place, he didn't immediately spot the car parked in a clearing about twenty yards ahead. Not like an old-time '57 Chevy, but a new BMW with a shiny cobalt-blue paint job.

The interior, with dark red upholstered seats and wood-grain paneling, contrasted sharply with the rugged surrounding of the forest. A red light blinked from the dashboard, indicating an alarm system. The license plate read Charlotte, North Carolina, the same city he had flown into from Boston.

His grandparents had a couple of neighbors living farther up on the mountain. The backside of their houses could be seen from the third floor attic, but his grandparents told him a route down didn't exist on this side of the mountain. The houses just gave the illusion of having neighbors, because a neighborly visit would mean a forty-five-minute winding drive down the mountain. So if not a neighbor's car, hikers were the only other explanation. The beauty of the place may have drawn them here. Maybe they hadn't realized they were on private land. Or they realized it, so they'd picked the odd parking place.

Something on the passenger seat caught his attention. He pressed his face against the window for a closer look. The sleeve of a Delta airline ticket, the same carrier he had flown, lay open. He cupped his face to block the glare off the glass and peered at the flight number. 417. His flight. He straightened, but before he could even think about what the ticket meant, he froze.

A massive black shape moved behind him. It snuffed out the glare on the glass with a bulk large enough to reflect across the entire window. He wondered if the warning about objects being closer than they appear applied to the reflections in a car window too. If so, he was in trouble. He stood as still as possible, the way he heard you should if you were ever in the woods and ran into a bear.

# 11
# FRIEND OR FOE

Nate's heart drummed against his chest so hard it constricted his breath. The bear stood behind him, no longer moving, but watching. Nate turned slightly for a better look. The bear shifted its weight. Nate squeezed his eyes shut, trying to stop trembling. Every neuron in his brain was firing like mad.

He could not outrun a bear. Nothing he could do would be better than a bear except think, but his mind was still in full panic mode when he needed to be calm and smart.

The bear had stopped about ten or twelve feet behind him. Its pumpkin-size head lifted into the air and sniffed loudly. Nate took long breaths and released them slowly; fearing even breathing sounds would provoke the bear. He did not dare take his gaze off the dark reflection in the car window.

Again, the bear sniffed the air. *Was it smelling something?* Nate remembered the food in his pockets and wondered if he could use it to escape.

The bear kept watch, and Nate watched him. He fumbled in his pocket and pulled out the granola bars. He slid a shaky hand up the side of the car and placed the snacks on top. As he inched toward the trunk, he sent out a silent prayer for the bear not to attack. The prayer must have worked because Nate glided all the way around to the passenger door before the bear moved toward the granola. A BMW between him and Smoky did not make him feel any safer.

The bear shook his enormous head and rose onto its hind legs with its massive bulk towering about eight feet into the air. The bear pawed a granola bar then used its sharp fangs to rip away the wrapping. It gulped down the bar in only a second then reached for the other one. Nate ditched the plan to run while the bear ate. The granola hadn't bought enough time for an escape. The bear would be on him in a flash. He needed a way to put more distance between them. And then he remembered the peaches.

Maybe if he threw a peach, the bear would run after it, giving him time to climb inside the car and wait until Smoky got bored enough to leave. If he blasted the horn, it might be enough to scare off the bear as well.

He pulled a peach from his pocket and momentarily considered using it to beam the bear. On second thought, if the throw didn't hurt the bear enough to make him leave, it might tick him off enough to make him attack. Nate nipped the idea and yanked the handle on the car door. *Stupid lock!*

The bear dropped to all fours and circled toward him. Nate circled the car too, determined to stay on the bear's good side, which, as far as he cared, was on the opposite side of the BMW. In a few seconds, he and the bear had exchanged places. Nate tested the passenger door. *Dang! He could not catch a break!*

Now at the driver door, the bear pawed the ground where Nate had stood then raised its head and sniffed the air again. Nate glanced at the cut on his hand. The blood had spread in a thin line from his palm to just beyond his wrist. Maybe bears smelled blood like sharks. *Except bears are mostly vegetarians, right?*

Once more, the bear moved in a circle toward him. Nate panicked. He hauled his arm back and threw the peach as far as he could. He didn't bother checking to see if the bear would oblige him and go after it. He turned and broke into a sprint, deciding to run, win or lose.

Immediately he slammed into something that materialized out of nowhere. He spun to the ground, catching only a blurry image before being grabbed by the arm and hauled to his feet. His back was pinned tightly against what felt like a chest. *Trapped.* He jerked away, only to be pinned even tighter before being given a quick shake. In the next second, he was whipped around and stared into the eyes of the bronze-faced man.

"Never run from a bear," the man whispered in a heavy accent.

"What?" Nate said, confused but not by the man's accent. What the heck was he doing here, holding him in a vice? He cast an anxious glance back at the car. The bear had not taken the peach bait.

"They are not puppies. They do not fetch," the man whispered again as Nate continued to sort out the mess he was in.

Nate's breath came fast and shallow. He had no idea where the guy came from or why, and he sure did not know how he felt about the guy's 9mm gun, currently pointed at the bear. For the moment at least, Bronze-Face was his best chance at surviving the bear, but…

"You… you're not going to shoot, are you? Because, I think they're protected," Nate said even though he was pretty sure it wasn't true. Still, he didn't want this guy to go all pistol-happy, and killing a bear for being hungry didn't seem right.

The guy relaxed his grip a little, as if he didn't trust Nate not to run. "We can try backing out of here. But if the animal charges, I must shoot."

That sounded fair, only the bear had reached their side of the car and did not act as though it planned on leaving. Maybe it was thinking about its next move.

Nate took a deep breath. "Okay, how about I scare it off," he suggested, feeling braver with back up by his side. "I don't think they like noise so if I act big and yell it might scare him away."

"Yes," Bronze-Face answered. "That would have been something to consider if you had not started feeding it first. I doubt if the bear would take you seriously now."

"Good point," Nate said. "You scare it."

Bronze-Face looked at him with a frown.

"I would do it, but like you said—" Nate started.

"Please, shut-up." The guy moved forward and stood between Nate and the bear. "Keep moving, but slowly," Bronze-Face ordered. "I will try to scare the animal. But if it charges, I will shoot."

The bear was doing a kind of zigzag walk toward them. Bronze-Face stood his ground. Nate watched from about six feet behind him. The bear stopped and rose onto his hind legs then pounded its chest with its paws. *That cannot be good.*

Bronze-Face spread his legs and shook both arms above his head. Nate had a pang of regret for suggesting the scare idea. *Was he crazy?*

The bear roared.

Bronze-Face yelled something in a foreign language, high pitched and shrill like a hyena cursing. Unfazed, the bear dropped to all fours, looking more menacing than before.

Bronze-Face took aim.

The bear lumbered forward.

Bronze-Face fired.

At the ear-piercing noise, Nate winced and looked down. A few seconds later, he felt Bronze-Face's hand on his arm.

"It is okay. It is over." The man sighed. "Please, let us go, before the animal returns."

*Returns? What?* He looked up. The bear was nowhere in sight. "You didn't kill it?"

"I fired a shot over his head. The noise scared him off, but he may come back. Let us go," the guy urged again.

"Yeah, sure," Nate agreed. "Let's go." He remembered the car. "Is this yours?"

The guy hesitated then nodded.

"You live around here?"

"No, it is a long story. I will explain, but we must move, yes?"

The guy no longer held the gun, but his loose fitting slacks had a bulge. Nate had heard about kids being abducted, but he didn't figure the guy as a creep. Still, there seemed to be too many coincidences for everything to be okee-doekee. *Getting in the car was a no-no.* But Bronze-Face thumbed his finger at the opening in the woods. "We should leave."

"Yeah," Nate said. He stood a few feet in front of Bronze-Face, who made no effort to catch up. Nate felt like a hostage being forced to march even though Bronze-Face was being all polite and nice. Nate took only a few steps before deciding to call the guy out. He turned and then stepped up to the man and met his eyes. Toe-to-toe, they stood at equal height, but the guy had about ten or fifteen pounds on him.

"What're you doing here?" Nate asked bluntly.

The guy glanced over his shoulders to the deep woods. "I would truly feel more comfortable talking in the open," he said and stepped away, taking long strides toward the clearing. Given no choice, Nate followed.

They reached the clearing where a light rain was falling from a clear-blue sky. Bronze-Face looked up with outstretched arms and smiled. "We are being blessed."

Nate had to admit, rain on a clear day did feel kind of magical. Somehow, it helped ease his suspicions, and he relaxed a little as Bronze-Face offered his hand.

"I am Abdi Ahmead."

Nate shook the guy's hand. Maybe he had been too scared to notice before, but now he caught a whisk of the tangy smell that seemed to come from the man. The scent was faint, but the same smell had been in his room yesterday morning. "Nate Daniels," he said slowly.

"I am happy to meet you, Nate Daniels."

"Yeah, likewise," Nate said, trying to figure out the guy's game. Something was up.

"Of course, you are wondering why I am here." Abdi bowed slightly, or maybe it was just a slow nod.

"Yeah, you were on the plane, right?" The guy would be hard to mistake for anyone else. His dark olive skin went with his black hair, but contrasted sharply with blue eyes.

"Yes." Abdi paused, seeming to struggle with something then continued. "I am not sure how much you need to know, but you have something I must retrieve. If you would please give me the USB device you found in your jacket, I will be on my way."

Nate's eyes narrowed. "How do you know what was in my pocket?"

"I placed it there," Abdi confessed. "I came here to recover it, but the USB is not where I left it. I am sorry to have involved you; however, I could not risk it being found. You have it, no?"

Nate thought about telling the guy he'd wasted his time. Explain how the pocket had a hole he'd been intending to fix. Nope, no USB here.

Now some of the odd things happening in the house made sense. Like blinds parting when they shouldn't and phantom shadows out his bedroom door. Abdi had already checked out the house. This explained the crumpled clothes in the suitcase. Abdi had been thorough. He had to know there was no hole in the pockets of the hoodie; heck, he probably had the missing hoodie. Abdi hadn't counted on the USB being found then propped up against a black phone and all but disappearing from view. But if Abdi had found what he wanted, he wouldn't be in the woods today, saving Nate from a bear. Nate felt he owed Abdi something and hesitated to lie.

"You sound all cloak and dagger, man. Like a Brad Pitt movie."

Abdi let out a long breath and gestured to the road with an open palm, suggesting they should walk. He laced his hands behind his back as they strolled in the light drizzle, surrounded by the smell of warm, wet earth. Abdi glanced at Nate sideways then fixed his gaze somewhere in the tree-covered mountains ahead. "I shall start from the beginning."

## 12
# RED ALERT

"You did what?" Hannah yelled. Nate jerked the phone from his ear. After telling her about giving Abdi the USB and about what Abdi said was on it, he expected her to be thrilled. *How often do you get to help a spy?* But Hannah kept quiet during the telling. He'd hoped her long silence reflected the awe the situation deserved, but apparently not.

"Yeah, I know. Cool, right?" he said.

"How could you? That's aiding and abetting a terrorist."

*Here we go.* "A spy who pretended to be a terrorist," Nate corrected.

"You do not know that! Maybe he lied to you."

"I believe him."

"Nathan, we need to contact the authorities and tell them the man they were looking for is here in North Carolina."

"What? No! We can't. They'll lock him away. He'll never get the information to the right people."

"Nathan, if they capture him and if his story is true, the people needing his information will verify he's a spy. He will be released. No harm done."

"No, Hannah, it won't work that way. Abdi's records were replaced with stuff that supports his cover. And now someone is trying to make his 'homegrown terrorist' cover permanent." Nate paused, expecting a smart-mouth reply. Hannah kept quiet, so he kept talking. "Only two people know the truth and one of them is missing. The other person is this general at the Pentagon. But he's never actually met Abdi. The proof of Abdi's spy activities is on the USB." Nate paused again and Hannah finally broke her silence.

"And you said he took the place of someone else who was supposed to be on the plane?" She sounded calm now, almost patronizing. "Yeah, see, Abdi got a note from his contact two days before they were to meet. Abdi was supposed to give the USB to his contact. But his contact said in the note that he was being followed. They couldn't risk a meeting." Nate stopped to get Hannah's reaction, but again she had nothing to say. He got the feeling her silence was generally a bad thing.

"Abdi said the USB would prove a plan to ambush American troops in Afghanistan and expose an enemy agent in the government. Only his contact knew Abdi had made it back to the States so Abdi stood a better chance of delivering the intelligence." Nate let his voice drop to a low whisper. "Hannah, somebody in the government is after Abdi and the flash-drive."

"But you said he needed to deliver the USB to the Pentagon, and yet he was on a plane to North Carolina." Her patronizing tone was obvious now. "Nathan, does that really make sense to you?"

"You don't understand. Abdi's partner planned to deliver it to the Pentagon. Abdi thought he stood a better chance delivering the flash-drive to MacDill Air Force Base in Tampa, Florida. Both the Iraq and Afghanistan wars were run from there you know," he said as if he hadn't just learned it two hours ago. "Abdi said some anti-terrorism operation is being run there now. Abdi tried to deliver the USB to MacDill and stay under the radar of someone he suspects is a Taliban mole at the Pentagon. Abdi planned to make a connecting flight to Tampa, but then federal agents stormed the plane. Now he thinks they know about him and reaching the general at the Pentagon is his last chance of stopping the ambush."

Hannah heaved a loud sigh as if she was about to do something against her better judgment. "Okay, did he give you the name of the general?"

"Yeah, but the general can't verify who Abdi is until he sees the USB. No one knows what Abdi looks like. That's the only reason they didn't catch him on the plane. They were looking for the guy whose place he took."

Hannah's silence was different this time. He could almost hear her thinking. "Give me the name of this general," she said. "I'll check your terrorist's story."

"Oh yeah? How're you going to do that?"

"General Towell owes my family a favor."

"You mean *the* General Towell? As in Desert Storm? Man! My dad served under him. Your family has that kind of clout?"

"My father had that kind of clout. It's a long story. Tell me who your terrorist says he needs to deliver the USB to, and I'll ask General Towell to arrange for me to speak with him," Hannah said as if she didn't realize what a big deal it was. "If this general can verify a U.S. undercover operative is missing from the Taliban, I'll believe him. Otherwise, I'm calling the authorities."

"Hannah, did you hear what I said about a big shot in the government not wanting the USB delivered?"

"Yes, Nathan. Remember, you have only your terrorist's word for that."

"No, there's a plant, a Taliban spy in charge somewhere up the chain of command."

"Again, you do not know that. Just give me the general's name and I'll get back to you."

"Abdi said it's a general named Kane," Nate told her.

"C-A-N-E?" Hannah asked.

"No, with a K."

"Fine." Hannah hung up. Did all girls have a kill button for thrill? But then again, Hannah could call up a five star general for a chat. *What kind of girl did that?*

****

Four hours after talking to Hannah, Nate sat in one of the porch swings, watching his grandparents play a game of Clubs at the wicker table. They all looked up at the sound of a car coming down the driveway. Hannah stuck her head out the car window and waved from the backseat. As the car pulled in front of the house, Nate could make out her brother in the passenger seat. A boy he didn't know drove. Surprised by their visit, he jumped from the swing and hurried down the steps to greet them.

Passengers and driver were out of the car and was standing on the walk by the time he reached them.

"Nathan, this is our cousin Jacob, and you remember William, don't you?" Hannah said.

"Yeah, sure." Nate bumped both boys' fists. "You guys want to come in for a soda or something?"

"Naw, man, I'm good," Jacob said then turned to Will and Hannah. "You guys got a ride home?"

"Thanks, Jacob, but we'll think of something," Hannah told him. "Have fun at work."

"You bet," Jacob said. "You know what they say. 'It's a happy kind of place.'" He waved to Granddad and Grandma then got back into the car, turned around, and honked as he drove toward the highway.

Hannah turned to Nate with a wrinkled nose. "Sorry to barge in like this, but we need to talk in person."

"Sure," Nate said. "Come on in."

They reached the porch where Hannah introduced her brother to Grandma and Granddad and apologized for the uninvited visit.

"Nonsense," Grandma said. "You're as good as family. Drop by whenever you like. Nathan, get our company some refreshments."

"Sure." Nate led them through the screen door and into the foyer, heading for the kitchen.

"We're fine, Nathan," Hannah said. "We don't want anything."

"I could go for something cold to drink," Will said.

"William, stop thinking about yourself for a minute. This is important. Nathan, in what room would your grandparents be least likely to interrupt us?"

"Ah, yeah, okay." He took her need for privacy to mean she had more news about the farm. "They spend most of their time in the kitchen because their bedroom and sitting room are by there. They use the music room for playing their old-fashioned records or for making phone calls. The study and library are on the other end. Granddad and I play chess there. He's just finished whupping my butt, so I'd say we have at least a day before a rematch. They hardly sit in the—"

"So," Will interrupted, "the study?"

"Yeah, probably," Nate said. Just by being Hannah's brother, Will made him nervous. He had a jumbo afro and his skin was the same shade as Hannah's, as were his features, but bolder. Taut muscles in the boy's arms showed some serious dedication to sports or workouts. Being an inch taller than Will didn't matter because no way could he take this guy in a fight; if say, Will was the kind of brother who bullied a guy for liking his sister.

"Let's go to the library." Hannah walked down the hall at a quick pace; the sound of her heels echoed off the marble until she reached the hardwood floor of the library. Nate and Will trailed behind her, occasionally eyeing each other like they were sizing the other one up.

In the few seconds it took them to follow Hannah through the door, she had taken a seat on the couch facing a giant brick fireplace with floor-to-ceiling bookcases on both sides. A second couch bumped against the first but faced out the windows with a view of mountains touching the clouds.

He and Will walked over and took seats in the two wing chairs facing her.

"This place is something," Will said, scanning the library. "What year was it built?"

"Not now, William," Hannah said. "Nathan, have you seen the news?"

"No, why?"

"Your terrorist is on it. By tomorrow, he'll probably be on the front page of every newspaper too. They've launched a manhunt for him."

"What? You ratted him out?" Nate shook his head in disbelief. "What happened to 'I'll get back to you'?"

"I didn't tell anyone." Hannah hung her head and lifted a hurt gaze in a poor-little-puppy-dog way. "I don't know how they found out, but he's in trouble."

Her sad eyes made him melt. "Oh, okay, right. Sorry. Well, what about Abdi's general? Were you able to get through to him?"

"No, General Towell wouldn't pass me through or answer any of my questions."

"Yeah? Well, I sort of figured," Nate said.

"I think General Kane is stonewalling General Towell, and he's doing the same to me. I can't believe it after all he said about calling him if we ever needed anything," she said in a huff.

"Cut the man some slack, Han," Will said. "There are probably all kinds of security clearance you need before he could even acknowledge a threat of any sort to you." Will faced Nate. "Your guy maybe telling the truth, but he's on his own. No one will back him up. He's screwed."

"So, wait," Nate said, turning to Hannah, "did the manhunt start before or after you called?"

Hannah dropped her head again. "I called right after we spoke before lunch. Two hours later, he was a special bulletin on the news. I'm sorry, Nathan."

"No, this isn't your fault. We should have figured this might happen. But there's still a chance he'll reach the Pentagon okay, right?" Nate said.

"I wouldn't take those odds," Will said. "The state is already at heightened alert, and the whole country is on terrorist watch. Every highway, airport, train station, and bus depot have raised their threat level. Even the Coast Guard has joined the search."

Hannah walked over to kneel beside Nate and took his hand. "We'll have to pray everything will turn out for the best."

Nate wanted to squeeze her hand but glanced at Will and folded his arms instead. "Yeah, thanks for coming out and telling me."

Hannah and Will exchanged glances. "Well, that's not the only reason." Hannah stood. "William is a history buff. He can help with the farm's mystery. I told him what I know; we could use another brain on this, right?"

"Sure, cool," Nate agreed. "I'd appreciate the help, man."

"So." Will stood and rubbed his palms together. "What have you tried?"

"Um, what do you mean?" Nate asked.

"Hannah said you think this house has secret places that may prove a connection to the Underground Railroad. So, what have you done to find them?"

"Well, since I got here on *Saturday*, and by the way, today is *Monday*, I've only found a stairway."

"So, you've been goofing off?" Will grinned.

Nate gave him a sneer of a smile and stood too. "Want to check-out the stairway?"

Hannah and Will had the kind of look Nate reserved for new gaming systems. "Of course," Hannah answered eagerly.

Nate led them upstairs to his mom's old room then down the secret passage to the small alcove.

"This doesn't seem like a hiding place," Will said when they got there. "Why keep a runaway in a stairwell? Most hiding places were cramped and not easily found. Like under floorboards or something. This one doesn't make sense."

"Maybe it leads to the hiding place," Hannah said.

"We have a bedroom on one end." Will turned to Nate. "Where does this come out?"

"The breakfast nook in the kitchen," Nate told him.

"Doesn't seem like much of a hiding place." Will stomped on the plank floor then tried to pry a couple of boards up. "Sometimes people made a space beneath floorboards to use as a hiding compartment, but this place doesn't seem to have one," he said when he straightened.

"Why would someone put a secret hideaway inside a hideaway?" Nate asked.

"Because if this is all there is to the stairwell, it doesn't support your Underground Railroad theory." Will said. "Secret stairways are in lots of old houses. They had all kinds of uses, including hiding soldiers, both Union and Confederate. Sometimes people used them to conceal illegal activities, or sometimes as a way to leave the house without being spotted by an unwelcome visitor. I guarantee you; someone looking for a runaway in a place like this would be looking for a hidden stairway. And they're not hard to find. So why hide runaways in a place that would be the first place a bounty hunter would search?"

"You're the history buff, you tell me," Nate said.

"Hannah said your great-grand was a genius architect or something."

Nate shrugged. "I guess."

"So maybe something in another part of the house can help us figure out what this stairway was meant for, because more than likely it's not a hideaway."

"So, he built it just for fun?"

Will hunched his shoulder. "If your great-grand was really a genius, and if he was a station master, then he would have known this place wouldn't conceal anything or anyone for long during a search."

"But he was a genius," Hannah said. "He used geometric angles to make rooms appear bigger than they were. It was a trademark of all his houses."

The same warm fuzzy feeling as the first time Hannah said Great-Gramps was brilliant came again. The spirit of Nathan Freedman the First was with them. And it was weird how the old ghost seemed to so all-gaga every time Hannah said something nice about him. Maybe Hannah's words made him think she understood something no one else did. Had her words hinted at a clue? And if Nathan Freedman's house had even deeper secrets, could they find them?

# 13
# HUNTING FOR CLUES

"I have an idea where to search for the cemetery." Nate shook off the spooky feeling of another ghost encounter and forced his mind back to Hannah and Will in the alcove. He showed them how the hidden latch worked before he led them into the kitchen and closed the cupboard behind them. "You guys want to take a hike? It's not far from where I met Abdi, but we should probably take some mace or something, in case we meet another bear."

"Bear?" Hannah said. "No thanks, I'll pass."

"Sure," Will said, "let's go."

Nate figured Hannah's skirt and low heels weren't meant for hiking. Still, it seemed rude to leave her behind while he went in search of the cemetery with Will. But if she *really* wouldn't mind …

"Maybe it's best if we split up," he suggested. "Will and I can check out the woods while you poke around the house."

"How do you think it would look if I searched your grandparents' place without you?" Hannah asked.

"Yeah, suspicious," Nate agreed. "But it would probably look suspicious even with me."

"Let's all check out the woods," Will said. "We'll just stay long enough to have a look around. What do you say?"

"I say no," Hannah said. "You two go tracking through the woods. I'll stay here and keep your grandparents company."

"Okay, that works for me." Will shrugged.

"Are you sure you don't mind?" Nate asked.

"Not at all. William can take pictures with his phone if you find anything important. It'll be just like I was there."

\*\*\*\*

Fifteen minutes later, they reached the pipe crossing. Nate pointed to the curtain of trees where he had met the bear in the prehistoric looking forest. "It's worth seeing, unless you're chicken," he told Will.

"Yeah? You wish, Goldilocks." Will moved ahead of him. "Let's go."

They followed the bent blades of grass still flattened from tire tracks. As they stood beneath the ancient looking trees, Nate puzzled over Abdi's car, still parked in the clearing. He turned his gaze toward the woods, almost expecting the spy to walk out. He tested the car handle and was surprised to find the door unlocked and the keys under the visor. Keys to a maxed-out car tingled his core.

"Is this his car?" Will asked, peeping into the window on the passenger side. "I thought you said he left." He stared suspiciously at the woods, like Abdi might be lurking there.

Nate broke the spell the keys cast by shoving them back under the visor. He closed the door and studied the woods again as well. "When he had me bring him the USB, he waited behind the oak tree near the back door. I saw him walk back this way, but I didn't see him drive off. He said it was urgent to deliver the USB to the Pentagon, so I don't think he's still here."

"Then how did he leave? You said he was alone, right?"

"Yeah. But maybe he ditched the wheels because he knew they would be looking for the car?"

"That would be smart, but he didn't know about the manhunt. No reason for him to be cautious."

"Maybe he figured it was coming. We don't know if Hannah's call started the manhunt. Things may have been already in the works."

"Say you're right," Will said. "Then I ask again, how else did he leave?"

"That road," Nate pointed back the way they came, "leads to the highway. He could have hitchhiked."

"Yeah, but that would be like leaving a trail of bread crumbs. Anyone who gave him a ride would be able to alert the feds to where he was heading."

"Maybe he reached his contact." Nate picked a twig off the ground then snapped off pieces and tossed them randomly. He could think best when he busied himself with something to do. "Maybe accused Terrorist #2 came and picked him up. There was no reason for him to hang around." Nate shrugged off an uneasy sense of something gone wrong and threw the last of the twigs. "Come on, I'll show you the grove we should plan to search."

On the trail above the stream, he figured now as good a time as any to clue Will about his feelings for Hannah. At least if Will decided to beat him up, no one was around to watch.

"Look, man," he started, "I want to be straight with you about something." He walked a few steps ahead then faced Will mano-a-mano.

"Shoot," Will said.

"Hannah is…uh, well…"

"Yeah, she's in perfect health," Will said. He grinned and continued walking as if he knew what Nate wanted to say.

"So, look," Nate said, jogging a little to catch up. "I think she's special and I respect her and everything."

Will didn't even glance back. "Han's bossy. Always has been, and she takes herself way too seriously. In fact, she takes everything seriously. You need to think about that."

"That's perfect," Nate said. "Because life is serious business. I respect her for that … like a lot."

Will stopped and faced him. His eyes had turned hazel in the bright afternoon sun and now they pierced Nate with a cold glare. Nature went suddenly mute because all Nate heard under the pinning gaze was the pulse pounding in his ears. *Crap, he is going to beat me up.*

"You need to think about it because Han doesn't play games. If you two ever break things off, and I mean *EVER*, you better make sure she's the one calling it quits." Will leaned closer until they were almost nose-to-nose. "Or else."

*Wow, really?* "No problem." Nate swallowed. "I wasn't even … I mean, yeah, sure. I wouldn't have it any other way." He hoped his mouth resembled the smile he intended. *Boy! And Will thinks his sister is the serious one.*

They walked in silence until they reached the trees with the opening like a gaping mouth.

"See, there," Nate said as they walked over and leaned into the gap.

"You might be right," Will said with a voice free of the threatening tone he used earlier. "This might be a good place to start." He stepped through the opening and turned in a circle as he took in the scenery. "Flatland and trees would guard a cemetery against ground erosion over time."

"And it feels peaceful here too," Nate said. "This is where I would put a cemetery I didn't want people to find."

"Well, they didn't necessarily want to hide it. We need to learn more about the history of the farm before we jump to any conclusion. But you're right; we should start the search here."

"Cool," Nate said, relieved the tension between them had passed. Despite Will's reaction to his liking Hannah, with Will's help in the search for the cemetery, he was more hopeful about finding Nathan Freedman's grave.

✶✶✶✶

They were back at the house forty-five minutes later. Grandma told them Hannah was up in the attic with Granddad.

"…Well no, not anymore." Nate heard Granddad's voice as he and Will climbed the stairs. "Ultima and I kept them on the shelves for a while, but we moved them to make room for our own collection. Those books are mostly about agriculture and farming matters. Of course," he said in his college professor tone, "book preservationists would frown on an attic as a home for the archive. 'Books like to live where you live', they would say. I suppose we should have given them to a historical society, but sentiment made us keep them."

They reached the top as Granddad closed the flaps of a box and nodded to the other end of the attic. "Let's see if we have better luck over there, shall we?"

He and Hannah crossed the room to boxes pushed into the corner. Granddad pulled out a pocketknife and ran the blade along the yellowing length of tape holding the flaps in place. He pulled the lid open, creating a small dust cloud as he reached into a box and declared success.

"Books," he said and offered the one he held to Hannah.

"Thanks, Mr. Freedman," Hannah said then waved Nate and Will over.

Granddad opened a second box and pulled out another book. "*The Rural Economic of Tobacco Farming*," he read. "Sounds about as dry as this attic."

"How old are these books?" Will asked, with a note of excitement creeping into his voice.

"They're all older than me." Granddad chuckled and handed Will the book as he walked to the stairs then headed down. "I'll leave you young people to sort them out."

"Let's check the dates on these." Will looked eager to dig into the musty boxes.

"Hold up." Nate fanned dust particles away from his nose. "Why would we want to do that?" He frowned and shook his head at Will. "And, Hannah," he turned the same puzzled face to her, "how did you get Granddad to bring you up here?"

Will took a seat on the grubby floor and continued as though Nate hadn't spoken. "Sometimes information was hidden in a book. Find a book that might have been around when the house was built, or shortly after. Comb through it for clues like a handwritten notation at the front or back. It might even be on a particular page, say, the same number as the house address."

"I don't think they had house numbers back in those days," Nate said. Will opened the cover of a book with reverence. Nate doubted he had even heard what he said and turned to Hannah. "Is he okay?" he whispered.

"He gets this way when he smells history," Hannah said. "Give it a few minutes and he'll forget we're even here."

"Yeah, right," Will said. "You two are helping me. Sit down and grab a book."

Hannah hunched her shoulder. She pulled an old ladder-back chair over to the boxes and took a seat. Will handed her a book that she placed on her lap on top of the one Granddad had given her then continued.

"When I mentioned to your granddad that my school's biology department had launched a campaign to collect all known writing of George Washington Carver, he invited me to go through these old books."

"George Washington Carver was a botanist," Nate said, deciding he'd been out voted and joined Will on the floor. "Not a writer," he added.

"He taught at Tuskegee Institute. He must have left behind some writings on farming. Maybe even documentation of his research," Hannah said.

"He did," Will put in absently. "*Help for Hard Times*, it was a pamphlet for Southern farmers."

"Yeah, okay," Nate said. "But we're not really interested, right? It's an excuse to search up here."

"Well, actually, as long as we're here ..." Hannah started.

"You two are yapping too much," Will snapped. "Shut-up and help me go through these books." Nate and Hannah exchanged glances that signaled the other to go along with the loony history buff.

The faint ding of the doorbell sounded downstairs. Nate wondered if visitors were a normal routine at the farm. The place seemed so isolated, but maybe his grandparents were more involved in the community than he thought.

"Ahem," Will cleared his throat loudly and bugged his eyes. "These books won't search themselves."

Nate laid the book he held flat on the floor and opened the front cover. "What are we looking for again?"

"I told you," Will said. "Find books that date back to your great-grand's time and look for clues like notations or anything out of place."

"All right. But let's move these boxes down to the library or something. This place is way too hot," Nate said.

Will nodded then stood, grabbing a box before heading for the stairs. Nate took the second box and followed behind Hannah. He reached the stairs and paused. Something about the attic seemed different.

He had come up here on his first day at the farm. The large attic had furniture, picture frames, lamps, trunks, and tons of other stuff his family had apparently cherished over five generations and couldn't discard even after the stuff had outlived its usefulness. But the first time he came up, three bicycles had stood propped up in a corner; now, there were only two.

While the missing bicycle answered one question, it spawned another. How did Abdi hope to reach the Pentagon in time riding a second-hand bike?

# 14
# THE PLANNED CONSPIRACY

"Well, we should think about getting home," Hannah said. Searching through the books had been boring enough, but Will made them treat each book as though the pages would crumble if they flipped them too fast. Humoring him had cost them time, and Hannah stopping to read sections of some books didn't help. After nearly two hours, they had only poured through about forty books.

"Let's not overstay our welcome," Hannah urged Will as he continued to turn pages. "We'll come back, okay?"

"Yeah, all right," Will agreed and got up from the thick throw rug covering the hardwood floor of the library. He stretched and then walked to one of the bookcases that flanked each side of the fireplace. "But you should stay on it." He turned to Nate. "You might want to do some research on the Underground Railroad too."

"Can't," Nate told him. "I don't have my computer with me."

"Hm …" Will drummed his fingers against the mantle. "If only you had another way to do the research, something like … oh, I don't know … books for example?" Will snapped his fingers. "Yeah, encyclopedias would be good." Will ran his hand across the spine of a row of Britannica encyclopedias with a sarcastic smile. "You see, before the Internet, they had these things called 'books' with all sorts of information in them."

Nate scanned the titles on the shelves for the first time. His grandparents had shelves full of reference books. He couldn't remember the last time he used a hardbound encyclopedia for research so he didn't wonder that the thought never occurred to him, still he was embarrassed the logic had escaped him.

"Yeah, sounds like a plan," he agreed then smiled awkwardly. "How are you guys getting home?" he asked, changing the subject and hoping to regain the appearance of intelligence. "I might be able to help you out there."

"How do you mean?" Hannah asked.

"I can drive you. Abdi's car is parked in the woods."

"You have a license?" Hannah asked, looking impressed.

"Not exactly," Nate admitted.

"A permit?" asked Will.

"Uh, no. But I'm a good driver."

"Look, slick, even if you can drive, you can't. Not without a license or at least a permit," Will said. Hannah nodded an eager agreement. They had to be the most straight-laced kids he'd ever met.

"Fine, so one of you drive to your grandparents' house, and we'll be all legal until I drive back."

"We do not have licenses, Nathan. We're fifteen."

"Both of you?" he asked, surprised, because seriously, they both acted way older. "You're twins?"

"It doesn't mean we're twins just because we're the same age," Will said. "Han could be adopted, or I could be eleven months older, or—"

"We are twins," Hannah said. "And I am the oldest." She got her purse from the end table. "I'll just have our grandparents send a cousin for us." Hannah took a cell from the purse. "No signal," she reported.

"Figures," Will said. "Too many mountains and not enough cell towers. Do your grandparents have a landline?" he asked.

"Yeah, at the other end of the hall. C'mon, I'll show you."

Nate led the way to the music room but stopped when he caught sight of a black Mercedes-Benz out a side window framing the foyer door. The car, parked behind his grandparents' Lincoln, reminded him of the kind the Secret Service used. If federal agents were here, it had to be about Abdi.

"Nice ride," Will said, looking out the window from the other end of the door. "Whose is it?"

"Feds?" Nate voiced his suspicion and his panic grew. He looked between Hannah and Will. "Abdi," he whispered.

"Oh, man," Will said, burying the fingers of one hand in his wooly mane. "Okay, what's our story? What do we do?"

"You two are ridiculous," Hannah said, shaking her head. "Why would federal agents be here?"

"Because Miss Butt-Her-Nose-Into-Everybody's-Business made a phone call," Will said.

"I did not make the phone call from here," she hissed at him. "And I never even mentioned Nathan or his grandparents."

"Okay," Nate stepped between them and signaled a time out. "Let's just figure out what to do."

"Do?" Hannah said. "We tell the truth. We show them the car and tell them everything we know."

"But I believe Abdi," Nate whispered. "He has important information to deliver. If they catch him, by the time all the smoke clears it'll be too late to stop the ambush."

"But you do not know if that's true," Hannah said. "He might be a terrorist with plans to sabotage our government. Could you live with yourself if that happens?"

"He's not a terrorist," Nate said.

Will turned another piercing gaze at him. "Han's right. You don't know for sure."

"Look," Nate said, "he didn't shoot the bear when it was the easiest thing to do. What kind of terrorist does that? And after he got the USB, he walked away. Would a terrorist leave a witness behind? No," he answered his own question. "Abdi is no terrorist. He's a good guy."

Will turned to his sister, "Did you tell him?"

"Tell me what?" Nate asked.

"Our dad died fighting Al-Qaeda in Afghanistan. If this guy is a terrorist, no way are we going to help protect him."

"Dang, guys. I'm really sorry," Nate said. "I can see why you're having a problem, Abdi being Muslim and all."

The twins looked at each other. "It's not about him being Muslim. This is about him possibly being a terrorist," Hannah said.

"We don't blame Dad's death on Muslims," Will said. "He died fighting Al-Qaeda and the Taliban. They're a Muslims sect, like the Ku Klux Klan is a terrorist group in our own country. Terrorists killed Dad, so if this guy is a terrorist, we'll do everything we can to help bring him down."

"But if it is true that he's helping to fight a war against terrorism, then we'll do everything in our power to help," Hannah added. "But we haven't met him, Nathan. We can only trust your judgment on this."

Will looked doubtful. "I'm not so sure about your judgment, but I'll go along with Han on this. But going around suggesting stuff like driving without a license makes your judgment look shaky."

"Yeah, well, I was just kidding about that." *Sort of.* "I appreciate what you guys are doing. Believe me, we're doing the right thing. I'd bet anything."

"You're betting people's lives. I hope you understand that," Will said.

"Because, Nathan, if you're wrong ..." Hannah started.

"Yeah, I know, I know, but I'm not. I can't be. We have to protect Abdi long enough for him to reach that general at the Pentagon."

"So, you got a look at what was on the USB, right?" Will said.

"No, there wasn't time. But Abdi said it laid out a planned ambush against troops stationed somewhere in the Spinjar Mountains."

"Spin Ghar Mountain Range?" Will questioned. "He told you that?"

"Yeah," Nate said. "Why?'

"That's where Dad's old platoon is stationed. Near Sikaram," Hannah said quietly. "Some of his men still stop by for visits when they're in the States."

"Oh, well, Abdi said the base was a big target because both American Special Forces and a British Special Project team operate from there," Nate said.

"Our dad was with Special Forces," Will said. "It's not general knowledge that a regiment of SAS is collaborating with a company of Special Ops."

Nate looked to Will. "So what's this SAS?"

"Special Air Service. Some of Britain's finest like American's SEAL. Special Project is a branch of the SAS."

"How do you guys know all this stuff?" Nate asked.

"Our dad's job made us high risk," Hannah said. "We've been stationed all over the world with him. He taught us about the different military operations and how to avoid being taken hostage since we were little."

"Wow, that's so cool," Nate said.

"Not really," Hannah said softly. "It makes you paranoid. We don't even carry ID because Dad always said it was like carrying your life history on a card and gave the bad guys too much information."

"Our dad was a hero." Will sounded like he wanted to change the subject. Nate thought he knew why. He couldn't imagine losing his dad.

"Yeah, sounds like it," he said. "But, his old regiment is in trouble. Abdi was undercover with the terrorist group planning the ambush of the base. They know something major is happening on that mountain."

"Then we need a way to warn them," Will said. "Do you think General Towell could get a message to them?" he asked Hannah.

"He could but I doubt he will. Not without more evidence to show the threat is real," Hannah said.

"How much time did Abdi say they have?" Will asked.

"He didn't say," Nate said. "But he was in a big hurry to reach the Pentagon. I know this is tough, but the best thing to do right now is to keep quiet and trust Abdi."

"Maybe Nathan is right." Hannah turned to Will. "If Abdi is the only person who can stop the ambush then we do not want to say anything to keep him from reaching the Pentagon. Let's hold off revealing anything awhile longer. In the meantime, I'll see if I can find out more."

Nate relaxed. "So we're all agreed, right?" His gaze darted between the twins until they both nodded. "Good." He took a deep breath to calm his nerves and led the way to the kitchen where he expected to find his grandparents being interrogated by government agents. Instead, he found them having tea with Reverend Ellis.

"There they are," Grandma said. "You kids remember Reverend Ellis, don't you?" Nate and the twins stood gawking at the scene for an awkward moment. They had prepped themselves for something much worse. Hannah recovered first.

"Yes, it's good to see you again, Reverend." Her flawless poise gave Nate another thing to admire about her. "I don't believe you've met my brother. William, this is Nana and Papa's minister."

"Good to meet you, William," Reverend Ellis shook the hand Will offered. "Hope to see you in church this Wednesday."

"Call me Will, and no offense, but I'm not big on being preached to."

"If you promise to come to church, I'll promise not to preach."

Will grinned. "You're a preacher who doesn't preach? Yeah, I'm almost tempted to come see how that works."

"Then it's a date." Reverend Ellis gave him a big smile and turned to Grandma and Granddad. "I appreciate your support on the matter we discussed. Thanks for the tea, but I should get going."

"Of course, Curtis. Keep us posted," Granddad said.

Reverend Ellis turned to Hannah and Will. "Can I give you kids a lift back to town?"

"Oh, Reverend, you're a godsend." Hannah beamed, which caused Nate to notice for the first time that the reverend wasn't too shabby to look at. He must be in his late twenties or early thirties. Nate hoped Hannah couldn't possibly go for someone so old.

He followed his grandparents as they led their guests to the front porch. They waved as Will and Hannah climbed into the reverend's black Mercedes and the three pulled off.

"I'll make those arrangements for the package Reverend Ellis needs delivered," Grandma said and went into the house. The screen closed softly behind her then Granddad turned to Nate.

"Did you kids find anything useful in those old boxes?"

"Well, we didn't finish searching through them. So far we haven't had any luck."

"Some of those books are as old as this house," Granddad said. "I remember watching them collect dust on the shelves when I was a kid. My father didn't care to read about how to farm, he just farmed. Of course, I never mustered enough interest in them. I hope your friends can find something useful in them."

"Yeah," Nate said. "We hope they'll be useful too."

"It's refreshing to see young people this interested in history. You know what they say. 'Those who forget their history ...'"

"... Are doomed to repeat it," Nate finished.

"Very good, Nathan. The only reason we don't repeat the atrocities of the past is because we have learned from them." Granddad patted his back and walked into the house.

Thunder rumbling in the distance threatened an evening storm as Nate thought about what Granddad had said. Nate's interest in the past only went as far as disproving a false report about his family's history. And if the clues he needed were hidden in a box of old books, then he intended to search them all.

# 15
# BOOK MARKER

Facing the French doors of his grandparents' terrace, the velvety black night caused the glass to reflect his image like a mirror. Nate tapped a finger against one of the rectangular shaped panes to scare off a lime-green moth the size of a fruit bat on the other side. The moth paid him no mind and continued its silent meditation of the light.

Seemed like every kind of creepy-crawly bug fluttered or crawled across the window. Beyond them, the blackest night he had ever seen revealed nothing more than the thin slit of a new moon and the occasional glow of a firefly. Once the sun went down in the mountains, going outside was like being swallowed up by a void. He had never thought about streetlights before, but now he missed having them around.

"Oh, the show is starting, Nathan," Grandma said from the settee she shared with Granddad. It was nine P.M. and time for *Secrets of the Dead*. Nate plopped down in an overstuffed chair that smelled of peppermint and settled back to watch the show. Chillingly, this episode told of a slave ship that went down off the coast of Florida over three centuries ago. Scientists were trying to piece together what life had been like aboard a slave vessel from the wreckage of the *Henrietta Marie*. When the show ended, Nate excused himself because he had some dead people's secrets to uncover too.

He went to the library and carried to his room one of the boxes of old books he and the twins had started to search through earlier in the day. He made a second trip for the other box then sat between them on the floor of his bedroom. Without Will around to hassle him about proper technique, he scanned books at a much faster pace.

Soon his eyes were too droopy to search the pages for the clues Will had said might be hidden inside. Turns out, research got a lot more boring when he did it alone. He kept nodding off then jerking his head up, trying to stay awake. Finally, he gave in to his body's need for sleep and went to the bed for a quick nap before having a go at the books again.

Sometime during the night, he woke to what sounded like soft footsteps thumping in an odd cadence. A rhythm of **thump**, pause, **thump**, pause, **thump** came repeatedly like someone hopping on one foot. The noise seemed to come from inside his room. He swung his legs over the edge of the bed and fought off the disorientation caused by waking from deep sleep. He wondered if the noise had been part of a dream as another *thump* erupted.

The lights were on, and he cast a drowsy gaze about the room. He caught sight of something happening on the floor and for a moment, forgot to breathe.

Adrenaline jolted him fully awake and he jerked his feet onto the bed as though they'd been dangling in an alligator pit. Had his room been transformed into a zoo, it would not have shocked him more than the sight just beyond his sleigh bed.

Books rose from a box, one after the other. They hovered in the air for a moment then dropped to the floor in single file. What was even freakier was the way they landed, in a straight line, about four feet from end-to-end. More books floated from the box and stacked themselves on top of the same row. When the box emptied, books rose from the second box to build an even taller wall. The pile grew until the height reached about six feet off the floor.

Nate sat not moving, glued to the bed, from shock mostly. *What the heck?* Then things got even stranger.

Books, neatly arranged in the bookcases flanking both sides of the fireplace, wiggled from their shelves. They glided into the air and drifted across the room to the construction site and then started a new row, connecting at a thirty-degree angle to the first. The thumping noise grew fainter as the books stacked higher. This stacking continued until the new row reached as tall as the first, but half as long.

No matter how real things seemed, this had to be a dream. He pinched the back of one hand to wake himself, but the sharp pain didn't change anything. Either what people said about not feeling pain in a dream wasn't true, or he was a witness to something that defied explanation.

The bedroom door opened with the squeaking sound he'd come to expect from the old hardware, then eerily, a line of books floated through like they hung on invisible strings. A set of encyclopedias he recognized from the library drifted over to the two rows of books on the floor. They piled themselves up at a sixty-degree angle against the shorter stacks until, together, the two rows looked like an upside down V capping the longest row.

He kept still, hardly breathing, until he realized about a minute had passed and nothing more happened. The room had gone still and cold as though some kind of consciousness was present and expected him to do something.

He eyed the books piled a few feet from him, as unmoving now as any other inanimate object. He wondered if he had gone bonkers or was hallucinating from lack of sleep. *Just breathe*, he told himself. *And think. Seriously, how could any of this be real?*

He decided the best way to handle a situation like this was to crawl under the covers until morning. When the bedroom door banged shut, he cancelled that plan.

Fear tightened in his throat now. He would yell if he thought his grandparent would hear him from the other end of the house.

He scooted out of bed and then skirted around the books until he reached the closed door. It wasn't bolted shut as he feared but opened easily.

He headed out the door but stopped on seeing the time glowing a bright green from the clock on the nightstand. Three o'clock. His grandparents must be sound asleep. Was it wise to wake old people so late?

Then he remembered the picture in the foyer and wondered if the wall of books would still be here by the time he ran downstairs to get his grandparents. Was it worth it? Would they say, 'Oh yes, those books do that all the time.' Was this another ghostly trick they already knew about? Reluctantly, he vetoed the idea of waking his grandparents.

He fingered his close-cropped head. Had his hair been long enough, he would be pulling it out in fistfuls. What was up with these books? One thing for sure, this ghost wasn't shy, so apparently it couldn't talk, or he would just say what he wanted. Nate got the feeling that both the books and the up-side-down portrait were connected and were meant to tell him something.

All things considered, it was a good thing the ghost couldn't speak because hearing a disembodied voice would freak him out more than he already was. Better to figure things out for himself. "So, yeah, I got this," he whispered, as much to the ghost as to himself, in case the ghost got any ideas about disproving his 'ghosts can't talk' theory.

Will had said messages were sometimes hidden in books. Maybe the ghost had heard and had gotten the idea. Nate circled the books, clueless to a meaning. Then an idea hit him. Maybe the top row of books spelled out the message. That's what he would do if he were the ghost. He pulled over the wood chair from the desk so he could see the top layer of books that ended an inch or so above his nearly six-foot frame. He placed the chair at the end of the longest row and stood on the seat for a bird's eye view of the pile.

Right away, he saw that books were placed with no regard to their orientation. Some were right side up while others were upside down. Some had spines turned to the wall, while other had spines turned away. He seriously doubted they held any message. He started to hop down then froze.

So caught up in finding a clue, he had overlooked the biggest one. He turned to study the books again. They did have a message. Just not the kind he had expected. No one would.

Looking at the stacks, he saw the shape. The books were arranged exactly like a giant arrow.

He jumped to the floor then walked in circles to release his mounting excitement. *But what was Great-Gramps thinking?* Didn't it occur to him the arrow would be easier to spot if the books hadn't been stacked so high? Why stack them into an arrow so tall? *Right!* It hit him. *That is the message!* The arrow didn't just point to the mantel, but a specific spot on the mantel. That had to be the reason for the height. His great-gramps wanted to draw attention to an exact spot on the fireplace.

Nate moved to the end of the arrow. He pushed the toy dinosaurs aside then ran a hand over the honey-brown finish of the mantel. Nothing felt funny about it. A slight layer of dust had accumulated since his arrival, but nothing felt out of place. Thinking a minute, he noticed the arrow ended at a height pointing to a location on one of the tree-shaped columns dominating both sides of the mantel.

He traced a hand up and down the decorative lines that twisted and turned in the intricate designed column. The elaborate sculpture depicted a great oak with branches, leaves, and ivy growing up a braided trunk. At first, he spotted nothing odd, but then his roaming fingers touched the smooth round surface of something hidden among a cluster of long curving leaves.

He traced his hand over the spot slowly. The circular shape felt out of placed among the long turns. The tiny mound rose from the carving too abruptly to be part of the design.

He used the chair to peer at the carved leaves midway up the column. A wood plug shaped like a small button rose out of the leaf cluster, just slight enough to be overlooked. He pried his short nails beneath the cap. It gave a little, and then he took a Swiss Army knife from his pocket. He extended the flat-head screwdriver attachment and gently worked the plug from the socket. The cap came loose without much effort, and to his surprise, a small roll of paper fell to the floor.

He didn't trust himself to pick up the roll. It had to be old, and Will had warned him about how delicate old paper could be. Suppose it crumbled in his hand, and it turned out to be something really important.

Three in the morning was too early to call Will for advice, but no way would he let his find lie on the floor until morning. He picked up the paper and unrolled it, but gently.

He held something important enough to have a hiding place. Would it answer all his questions about the farm? He crawled back into bed feeling like a kid who had just found a treasure map. And maybe he had.

He laid the paper flat on the bed, then held it in place by spreading his fingers wide along the ends. He placed his pocketknife on the top of the paper to hold it in place while keeping his finger on the bottom edge. He read the writing once, then read it much slower a second time. This definitely meant something; he just didn't know what.

# 16
# CODES

He let the paper curl up again then placed it in a drawer of the nightstand. He got off the bed and returned books to the bookcases and to the boxes. When he finished, he shoved the boxes into his closet then made several trips to the library, returning all but the U through W encyclopedia he needed for research.

The paper was a note, and it had to be about the Underground Railroad. It read like a code. Even though he thought he knew what parts of it meant, he couldn't be sure. Learning more about the Railroad might help make the meaning clearer. Way too excited to sleep, he settled into the wing chair in a corner of his room and read.

The encyclopedia's account of the Underground Railroad was brief, so maybe learning about the conductors who ran the Railroad would yield more information. He went downstairs again to the library and found encyclopedia volumes with information on some of the conductors he already knew. John P. Parker, Harriet Tubman, and Peg-Leg Joe— all had risked their lives time and again and made some huge sacrifices. He wondered about the many other conductors who hadn't made their way into the pages of a book. How many of their stories had gone untold? And what about the countless station masters along the way like William Stills, and maybe if the note he found meant what he thought it did, even his own great-gramps.

Nate couldn't imagine being asked to risk a punishment of imprisonment, enslavement, or death in order to help another American live free. Yet station masters and conductors had done so all the time.

How many of his generation would risk that? Would he? He didn't know. Maybe no one knew the answer to the question until faced with making the decision.

Lost in books and his own thoughts, he forgot about the time. When he finally looked up, daylight was streaming through the windows of the library. Through the beveled pane glass, the mountains were visible once more in the distance through a haze of early morning fog. He stood on cramped legs and stretched before he switched off the lights and climbed the stairs to his room. He slept until Granddad woke him at eight-thirty for breakfast.

Nate hadn't bothered undressing for bed, but Granddad didn't comment on the jeans and T-shirt he still wore. He just raised a curious brow before leaving the room. Now Nate longed for the sleep he had abandoned during the night and groggily peeled out of bed to grope his way downstairs to the kitchen.

He slumped into a chair at the table and shoved a couple of forkfuls of breakfast into his mouth before asking, "Do your books ever do anything funny?" He yawned but was too tired to put energy into covering a mouth full of cheese grits. He squinted in the direction he assumed his grandparents sat. "Morning," he added in case he had forgotten to say it before.

"Good morning, dear," Grandma said. "Are you sure you're awake? That's a very odd question."

Nate looked at her through the narrow slits he allowed his eyes to open. "Do they?"

"I'm afraid we weren't able to ascertain any books inclined to do stand-up comedy," Granddad said. "The ones we have just stay put until we come to read them."

"Funny," Nate said. "So, beside the Nathan Freedman picture, it would be really weird if stuff started moving on their own around this place?"

"Nathan." Grandma looked as though she intended to check his forehead for a fever. "What makes you say something like that?"

"Because last night, the books me and the twins took from the attic and the ones from the library hooked up in my room and made this giant arrow that pointed to a place above the mantel that hid a secret note." He caught his breath and shifted his gaze between his grandparents, trying to read their expressions. "Really, they did that."

"Books just piled themselves into an arrow?" Granddad asked.

"Honest, Granddad."

"Well, dear, that is a new one. We've only known the ghost to disturb the Nathan Freedman picture," Grandma said.

"But it really happened," Nate said.

"Where's the note?" Granddad asked.

"So, you believe me?"

"We have no reason not to believe you, even if you only had a very vivid dream. But, as they say, 'the proof is in the pudding.'" Nate turned a baffled look at Granddad. What the heck did that mean? Was there pudding?

"Can we see the note, dear?" Grandma said.

"Yeah, I'll go get it." He hurried to his room feeling wide-awake. He took the note from the nightstand very gently, then returned to the breakfast table. Grandma cleared the dishes so that they could cram their chairs around the table and read the note together.

*When the North Wind blows*

*Find the falling snow*

*Seek out the gray snake*

*On its back lies the gate*

*Keep your eyes to the sky*

*As the moon passes by*

*The brightest light you'll see*

*Is the guide you must heed*

*Persevere and keep hope*

*Help lies upon the Northern slope*

"Quite interesting, isn't it?" Granddad said. "Not sure it makes a lot of sense though. Where did you say you found this, Nathan?"

"Above the mantel in my room. The book-arrow pointed right at it."

"That was the original master bedroom," Grandma said. "I imagine because it has the best view in the house and allowed Nathan Freedman the First to keep an eye on his property."

"So, do you think Nathan Freedman put it there?" Nate asked.

"Well, that's hard to say. It has no date, but it appears old," Granddad said. "But any past occupant of the house may have placed it there."

"I think it's written in codes," Nate said.

"Yes, maybe it was once part of a child's game. My father and uncle grew up in this house. As did my sister and I. Kids had to be pretty creative to entertain themselves around here. Perhaps that spot wasn't always a secret and had once been a part of a scavenger hunt."

"Did you know about it?" Nate wished he could ask them straight out if they thought the note had something to do with the Underground Railroad. Except that was too close to the subject they kept trying to avoid, and he had promised his dad he wouldn't upset them.

"No, I don't recall ever knowing that about the mantel."

"Well, I'm going to figure out what this note means," Nate said.

"That's fine, dear. You know, there were once rumors that the Underground Railroad ran through here on a regular basis. Who knows, maybe you've found something left behind from that time."

He couldn't believe Grandma had said it, but Granddad furrowed his brow.

"People say a lot of things about this house. You'll need to have more than a deteriorating note to prove any kind of a connection."

"I know, but it's a start."

"Yes, it is a start," Granddad agreed. "And if it is a code, figuring it out just might improve your focus and thereby your chess game."

Nate grinned at the dig. "Just wait. You're going down," he threatened.

"Actually, your grandmother and I are going to drive into town and pick up a package for the reverend. We can drop you off at the Greens while we run our errands if you like."

As much as he wanted to see Hannah, this was his chance to check out the woods without worrying his grandparents. He knew they wouldn't be okay with him hiking through the woods alone, but he needed to continue his search for the cemetery, and with any luck, find another link to the Railroad.

"That's okay. I'll just hang out here and work on solving this."

"Are you sure, dear? You can bring the note with you. I'm sure William and Hannah wouldn't mind helping you figure it out."

In fact, Nate was counting on the twins helping with the codes, but not today.

"That's okay, Grandma. I'll work on it alone for a while first."

"All right then. We'll be back in a few hours." Grandma stood and walked into their bedroom then came out a minute later wearing a hat and gloves. Granddad jingled his pockets and pulled out a ring of keys. The ring had about a dozen keys hanging from it. Nate wondered what his grandparents did with all those keys because he had never seen them lockup anything.

"Nathan," Grandma said, "will you please tidy the kitchen while we're gone?"

"Sure, Grandma." He followed them to the foyer and out the door to the porch. He stood watching them drive away for a moment then went into the house.

He entered the foyer then looked back toward the driveway with a frown. Odd, his grandparents were driving thirty-five miles into town to pick up a package for the reverend. Except, the reverend was already in town. Why couldn't he pick up his own package? He shook his head, dismissing the thought as quickly as it came and ran up the stairs to dress for the hike.

# 17
# NEIGHBOR

He had sprayed himself with OFF and tucked the legs of his cargo pants into a pair of Granddad's work boots before leaving the house. In one of his pants pocket was a can of bear repellant from a back porch shelf. He had a red marker for marking trees and rocks to help find his way home if he got lost.

Reaching the yawning mouth of trees, he felt more prepared than on his first visit. He stepped between two large trees that formed an entrance. It was time to search for Great-Gramps' grave.

The woods were big and confusing. He vowed to find a real compass the next time he tried something like this. Once he got his bearing, the search became his prime focus for two hours, but he still couldn't find anything that resembled a cemetery or a grave.

He wasn't ready to admit defeat and hiked up a woodsy trail that led further up. He froze when a zooming sound came from somewhere overhead. He listened for a moment then climbed a bit higher, hoping for a better view. The only things in sight were more trees, shrubs, and wild vegetation growing up an incline.

The mountains echoed the sound so that it seemed to come from everywhere. As soon as he heard a zoom from one place, the sound bounced in another direction. Judging from the stray odor of engine oil and the increasingly loud voo-vrooms, something fast was getting closer.

The undergrowth grew up to his waist in places and did a good job hiding whatever blazed a path toward him.

He imagined a large prehistoric bumblebee, one with a damaged wing and causing an uncontrollable crashing through trees. All the weird stuff that happened since coming to the farm made him expect the unexpected.

Seconds later, the sound of swooshing branches and tree limbs snapping seemed to backup his bumblebee theory. A swift movement rushed across the hills a few yards above him, and then a bright flash of yellow burrowed through a thicket of giant ferns. He jumped out of the way as an ATV skidded out of control past him. The all-terrain-vehicle flipped on its side and slammed into a downed log about twenty feet away. *What the heck?*

He ran to the slight figure sprawled on the ground and knelt on one knee to touch the shoulder.

"Hey, you okay?" A helmet covered the face so he couldn't tell if the person's eyes were open or shut. He gently shook a shoulder. "Hey?"

"Ow." The rider pushed up onto an elbow and then struggled to pull off the helmet.

"Sorry," Nate said, standing and stepping away.

"Not talking 'bout you. That spill hurt. Good one, wuzn't it?" The rider freed his head then placed the helmet on the ground. He stood, dusting leaves and twigs from a pair of blue jeans and a yellow windbreaker.

Nate frowned down at him. "You meant to crash?"

"Co'rse not. Took a curve too fast and went off the path is all. Didn't break nothing though," the driver said with obvious admiration of his exploit.

"You got lucky," Nate said.

"Luck got nothing to do with it," the driver said. "Sheer skills what done it."

Nate studied the driver. Scary stuff coming down a mountain so fast, but the kid didn't even seem fazed. The fall had to hurt, but no trace of pain showed on the pale face topped by a mop of unruly sandy hair falling into brown eyes.

"How old are you?" Nate asked.

"Twelve, you?"

"Fifteen. You're pretty tough for twelve. Are you sure you're okay?"

"It smarts a bit, but it won't kill me." The kid gave him a puzzled look. "Never seen you 'round bouts here before."

"Yeah, I'm staying with my grandparents for the summer." He pointed in the direction he hoped was the farm. "What about you, where did you come from?"

"Your grandparents are Miz Ultima and Professor Freedman?"

Nate had never heard Granddad referred to as professor. "Yeah, you know them?"

"We're neighbors." The boy pointed up the mountain. "My dad took classes from your grandpa long time ago."

"Oh, yeah?" That explained the professor bit. "But my grandparents said there wasn't a road down from this side of the mountain."

"There ain't, 'cept for the trail me and my brother built for riding."

"You built a trail?"

"Yup, this side of the mountain is wilder. Loads more fun."

"Yeah, fun. You know there're bears in these woods, right?"

"Not to mention mountain lions and wolves," the boy said. "But they don't like noise. They'll leave if they hear you coming. They don't hunt people. Just make shur never to feed 'em."

"No," Nate said. "Wouldn't want to do that." He scratched the back of his neck self-consciously. "So, you roam around the woods a lot?"

"Yup, during the summer me and my brother u'sta ride down here."

Nate's spirit lifted at hearing this. "Have you ever seen a grave or cemetery?"

The kid stuck out his lower lip and shook his head. "Ain't no cemetery in these woods. Not even an old Indian burial mound." The boy kicked his heel into the ground and shoved his hands into his pockets. "Why would there be?" He looked at Nate. "That's what 'chur out here looking for?"

"Yeah, it was just part of a theory." He couldn't help being a little disappointed. For sure, two ATV riders would have run into a cemetery if they spent their summers riding through the woods. "Where's your brother?" He asked to change the subject.

"I don't know. With his girlfriend I s'pose. He's fifteen now. You gotta girl?"

"Nah," Nate said.

"Good, cuz' they ain't nothing but trouble."

"Yeah? Talk to me in a couple of years, kid."

"I'm telling you, girls ain't never gonna be my idea of fun. This here is fun." The boy jerked a thumb toward the ATV. "Hey, you wanna take a spin?" He tapped Nate's stomach with the back of a gloved hand and nodded at the ATV still lying horizontally against the log.

"Sure, do you think it still runs?"

"Heck, that spill wuzn't bad 'nough to bust nothing up. C'mon, I'll give you some pointers. Wha'chur name anyway?"

"Nate." He reached out and shook the kid's hand. "You?"

"Billy. Here, you betta take the helmet." The kid reached down and picked up the helmet then crunched his face as though something unpleasant just occurred to him. "Second thought, you betta not try riding 'round here. Trees don't move for you."

"I guess not," Nate agreed.

"There's a road though. It's not far from here. You can practice on it."

"Yeah, the dirt road at the bottom of the hill? I've seen it. There's a stream to cross before reaching it, and then a deep slope to maneuver down to the road. I don't see how we can get the ATV down that way."

"Shur we can. That creek's not deep and the slope evens out a bit if you know where to cross."

"Sounds like you know your stuff." Nate smiled and punched the kid's arm. "Let's do it."

They waded through the brook, pushing the all-terrain vehicle between them. The slope leveled out just as Billy said it would. From atop a ridge, they spied the road below along with something that caused Nate to step behind the low hanging branches of a pine. He tugged Billy and the ATV out of sight too. Nate bent low, hoping the men at the bottom hadn't spotted them on their perch.

"Wha'cha doing?" Billy asked.

Nate nodded to the road. "I think those guys are federal agents," he whispered. "They must be here to check out the car."

"Your grandparents' car?"

"No, someone abandoned a car in the trees on the other side of the road."

"So? How come federal agents care 'bout that? I mean, your grandparents might, but how come federal agents do?"

"Have you heard anything about a terrorist on the news?"

"For real? They think the car belongs to the terrorist? Right here? In these woods?"

"Yeah, they must have used the car's GPS to track it."

Billy looked around with wide eyes. "A terrorist is in these woods?" he whispered.

"No," Nate told him. "He's long gone."

"How you know?"

"Well, that's a long story. But trust me, he's gone."

"So, maybe you should go down there and tell 'em."

"Nah, things don't work that way, Billy. We need to keep low and hope they leave."

"What won't work which way?"

Nate turned to him and considered for a moment what to say. "Well, Silly Billy, I don't believe we've reached a point in our relationship where we share those types of secrets."

"Well, Mate Nate, if you don't want me to plow down this here hill and tell 'em you got some info they might find interesting, you betta start talking."

"Whoa." Nate's eyes widened at the boy's sudden savvy. "So you're smart. How come you sound like a country bumpkin?"

"It puts snobby city folks off their guard. Now talk."

Nate rolled his eyes. *Outwitted by a kid.* "Okay, look. This will sound crazy, but the terrorist's name is Abdi, only he's not a terrorist. He's a

United States operative with important information to deliver to the Pentagon." Nate studied Billy for any sign he was getting through, but the kid had a poker face. "Someone, maybe the boss of those men down there, wants to stop him from doing that. Do you believe me?"

"It sounds like a spy movie. You fooling me?"

"You know, I said the same thing when Abdi explained it to me, but I have my reasons for believing him. And sorry, I didn't mean anything by country bumpkin."

"Shur, I didn't mean to call you snobby." Billy sat back on his heels, looking as if he was trying to decide what to do. "You shur he's not still 'round here?"

"Positive."

"Then okay. I won't say nothing."

"Thanks." Nate glanced back the way they came. "So, no practice today. We better get you back up the hill."

"Okay, you can call me when you want a lesson. You got something to take down a number on?"

"I have a marker." Nate pulled the bear repellant from his pants pocket. "Write your number on this can."

Billy took the marker and the can and grinned as he wrote. "This here spray ain't gonna work 'gainst no angry bear. I reckon it's fine for spraying bears what wanders into your yard since it'll hit 'em from 'bout twenty-five feet away. But the best way to handle a bear in the wild is to keep your distance from 'em. Just remember, they're usually mo' 'fraid of you."

"I'll remember that," Nate said, taking back the can and marker. "You can call me if you want. Do your parents have my grandparents' number?"

"Yeah, I'll call you." He tilted his head as if he had reached a conclusion. "I'll keep your secret 'cause we're buddies now, okay?"

"Yeah, we're buddies," Nate agreed. "Let's get you home."

# 18

# RUNAWAY

The agents were gone by the time he returned to the ridge. He hunched low as he slipped down the hill and ran across the road into the woods. Abdi's car was still there, and Nate wondered if the agents were setting a trap, camouflaged and hiding behind the bushes and trees.

He studied the woods for any unexplained movements then realized how suspicious this made him look. He faked a puzzled expression in case someone was watching and circled the car like he had just come upon it for the first time. A few minutes passed without anyone challenging him, and he decided agents would have come out of hiding to question him by now. When he thought about it, there was no reason to keep watch over the car. The BMW's location could be tracked through the GPS if someone were to move it. Still, no way had the agents given up on investigating this place or the car. They probably had people at key points to watch the comings and goings on the mountain. Maybe they were waiting for backup to arrive. If they knew the car belonged to Abdi, there might even be agents at the house wanting to ask his grandparents questions about a terrorist's car on their property. He turned and rushed to the farm, hoping this wasn't so.

He eyed the back porch wearily as he approached, afraid agents were already inside. Anyone could walk into his grandparents' never-locked doors. He really needed to talk with them about that. He entered through the kitchen and then went to the foyer. The view out the window showed an empty driveway, yet he was on edge until he searched the house and declared an all clear.

At one o'clock, his grandparents still were not back. He went downstairs to tidy the kitchen the way he had promised and tried not to worry. At two-thirty, he decided it was time to worry. Suppose agents had taken his grandparents while he was out and were holding them for questioning? Could federal agents do that? Should he call his parents?

He dialed his mom's cell from the music room. Unable to get through, he called his dad but got the same out of area message. Now he knew why Mom wouldn't give up their landline. It was the only way to get a sure connection through from the mountains. He dialed the house and got the answering machine. To avoid worrying them, he left a message that he had called and for them to call back if they got a chance.

He slumped in the chair and jumped when the phone rang a moment later.

"Oh, Nathan, there you are. Where have you been? We were worried."

"Hi, Grandma. I was worried about you too. Are you guys all right?"

"We're fine, dear. This errand is taking longer than we thought because of all the roadblocks they're putting up. We've been pulling into gas stations and calling. Why haven't you answered the phone?"

"Sorry, I went for a walk," he answered, trying to sound calm. "Did you say roadblocks, Grandma?"

"Yes, dear. People from the government are positioned every mile or so."

He twisted the phone cord in his grip. "Did they say why?"

"I'm afraid they think one of those Taliban terrorists is somewhere in the area. We want you to lock the doors and stay inside, Nathan."

I will, Grandma." Agents were keeping watch on the mountain as he suspected. "How long will it be before you guys get here?"

"We're on our way now, but with security checks every other mile, it might take awhile."

"Okay, can I do anything?"

"Just stay close to the phone in case we need to reach you again."

"Sure, Grandma."

"Good, we'll see you soon. Bye, dear."

"Bye, Grandma."

He decided the house needed securing because of the agents, not Abdi. He locked the front door in the foyer and then headed for the back. He turned the deadbolt on the kitchen door just as he spotted a shape moving in the tall hedges beyond the backyard. Were agents really hiding in the bushes? He double-checked the lock then pulled down the shade that topped the two-foot pane of glass on the mahogany door. Double-hung windows behind the breakfast nook had shades that he pulled down too. As he headed to the dining room to close the drapes, a rattle of the kitchen doorknob stopped him in mid-stride. A tap-tap came next.

He stared at the door. Were agents testing the lock as a security measure or something? Had the tap been a knock? He walked to the door and stood to the side as he lifted the edge of the shade just enough to peep out. *What the?*

He hurriedly unlocked the door and opened it wide enough to let in the man who was too thin, as his mom would say, to cast a good shadow. Nate closed the door quickly and locked it again.

"Abdi! What are you doing here?"

Abdi's anxious gaze darted around the kitchen. "You are alone?"

"Yeah, my grandparents are out. Abdi, federal agents were in the woods!"

"I know. I saw them."

"They found your rental."

"That was inevitable." Abdi's blue eyes were wide with the type of focus trapped animals had. Never had Nate seen eyes so intense. "The car is of little importance now. They have blocked the roads. I had to turn around. There is no way out of the mountains."

"But, Abdi, you wouldn't have made it all the way to D.C. on a bike anyway, right?"

"I needed only to travel beyond the mountain so as to make a phone call and find assistance. My phone is secure, but a connection does not work inside your mountains," Abdi explained. "Now assistance cannot come, and I am unable to leave the mountains without it."

Nate could feel the man's fear and felt a little fear too. "What are you going to do?"

"Nate Daniels, I need your help."

"But, I don't know what I can do. I'm just a kid."

"It is my fault you are this much involved, but I must ask you to become even more so."

"What do you mean?"

"I need a place to hide. Will you help me?"

Nate nervously ran a hand over his mouth then across his smooth head. "Ah, man. This is crazy."

"I understand. I have asked too much." Abdi reached into his shirt pocket and pulled out the USB. "I will turn myself in, but it is imperative that you find a way to deliver this to General Kane." He took Nate's hand and placed the USB in his palm then pressed his fingers closed around it. "Will you make that promise, Nate Daniels?"

"Abdi, I don't know how." As soon as he sad it, he realized this wasn't entirely true. Hannah knew a general who could help make it happen. Nate believed Abdi when he said someone didn't want the USB delivered, so this didn't seem like a job for a kid. It needed Abdi, who was qualified to deal with any obstacles that might come along the way. But Abdi needed help if he was going to outsmart a federal agency already on his tail.

Nate suddenly understood how Great-Gramps must have felt, doing what he did even if it was against the law. Great-Gramps had followed his convictions and became a station master. Now, Nate had to decide if he could do the same.

His insides turned to Jell-O at the enormous consequences of getting involved, but he pushed those doubts and fears aside. Right now, he only had to hide Abdi. Take one-step at a time, and if there were consequences, they would be dealt with later.

Already a plan churned in his head. The plan was crazy. He would need to get some newfound friends to go along with a wild scheme. Still, if it worked, Abdi had a chance.

"Abdi, you have to deliver this," he said. "You're our best chance, but I'll help." He handed the flash drive back to Abdi.

Abdi's intense eyes softened a bit. "I am forever in your debt." He bowed, and Nate repeated the gesture.

He took in the man's slim form. "There's spinach manicotti left over from last night's dinner. I'll warm you some." He walked to the fridge and tossed Abdi a soda. "Is that okay?"

Abdi popped open the can and took a gulp. "Very refreshing." He nodded and smiled in a way that made Nate think he wasn't talking about just the cola.

Nate pulled out the tray of manicotti then scooped four onto a plate. He was about to microwave the food when the phone rang.

"Be right back." He dashed to the music room and picked up the phone on the fifth ring.

"Hi, sweetie, we got your message. Is everything okay? We saw the news. What's going on down there?"

"Hi, Mom. Everything's fine here. Grandma and Granddad are doing some shopping, but we're all good."

"Why did you call, honey?"

"No reason, I just miss you."

"Ah, that's so sweet. I don't know why I'm having such a hard time believing it. Really, Nathan, what's going on?"

"Mom, I told you, I just miss you."

"Okay, fine. Then tell me about the roadblocks. Are there any near the farm? How close is that crazy terrorist supposed to be from the house?"

"Don't worry. He's miles away."

"Honey, if you see anything suspicious, you lock the doors and hide in the secret stairway until Mom and Dad get home."

"Oh, yeah. I will, Mom. But I should get going. I have some chores to finish. Say hi to Dad for me."

"I'll have him call when he gets home. Bye, baby."

"Bye, Mom."

Walking across the foyer, a gust of wind blew past him from the Nathan Freedman picture frame. The air chilled him and once again, the picture of Nathan Freedman turned up-side-down.

"Not now, Great-Gramps. I'm a little busy." As though answering, the picture righted itself, but then flipped up-side-down again. It repeated this three times before Nate decided to ignore the antics and returned to the kitchen.

Abdi had devoured the plate of food and looked at the leftovers in the tray as though he could eat more.

"Abdi, we should probably get you out of sight. My grandparents could be back anytime now. You can eat some more in the stairway, okay?"

"Of course. You are wise." Abdi walked to the china cupboard and released the latch hidden inside the door. The passageway opened but not as wide as Nate's mouth.

"You know about that?"

"I was in the house the first day you found the hidden stairwell."

"Wait ... you were the shadow? I thought you were a ghost!"

"I was in the stairwell, yes. However, something else was with us too. I felt it. Cold, like death."

"You pushed me!"

"On my honor, I did not."

"Then what did? I get that this house is haunted and all, but why would a ghost push me?"

"Perhaps the ghost was only helping you find the way out."

It made sense. The ghost was trying to help him escape? "But why didn't it just push you."

"Perhaps it did not wish to push me down the stairs, and for that I am extremely grateful." Nate wondered if his great-gramps hadn't pushed Abdi because he'd judged Abdi as an honorable man. Did ghosts know about stuff like that?

"Okay, I hope you have his seal of approval," Nate said, "because you need to get in there and hideout."

They entered the stairway and climbed to the middle landing. Nate grabbed Abdi's arm when he headed for the top.

"Hold on, you should probably stay in the middle. If someone finds this place, it would be better to be in the middle so you can run either up or down."

"If they find this place, I think they will have both exits covered, but you are right. It is best to remain in the middle," Abdi said.

"We should probably turn off the lights too. You stay here. I'll go get some flashlights." He went down the steps and hurried to the laundry room. He took two of the flashlights his grandparents kept there. Passing through the kitchen again, he grabbed a bunch of bananas and tucked an apple under his arm. When he returned, Abdi was sitting on the floor of the middle landing. Nate switched off the alcove light on his way up and flipped on a flashlight. He handed Abdi the second flashlight then killed the light on the middle landing. He stepped around Abdi before giving him the fruit. Nate leaned back against the wall and slid to the floor. Just as his rump hit the bottom, the wall behind him shifted inward.

# 19
# UP-SIDE-DOWN

Abdi jumped to his feet before Nate could fully take in what had happened. Abdi pulled a gun from beneath his shirt and trained it on the wall as if he expected someone to pop out.

"Easy." Nate pushed off the floor with one hand and turned an open palm to him. "This isn't a trick," he said, meeting the man's eyes. "I think this is what I've been looking for." He turned to study the wall with giddy excitement growing inside. "See, these stairs are a decoy. This!" He aimed the flashlight at the crack. "This must be the real hiding place." He turned to Abdi with a big grin. "We should check it out."

Abdi moved his flashlight across the wall then nodded. "Perhaps fortune smiles on us."

"Yeah, come on." Nate pushed against the wall until it turned inward, revealing a slight doorway. He guided the flashlight beam to the floor and stepped inside then moved forward so Abdi could follow.

Abdi entered then turned his flashlight on the opening and pushed the entrance closed. He studied the door. "Here," he said, shining the flashlight on a metal rod held in place by two clamps. "This goes into that hole. It is the lock."

"Okay, lock it," Nate told him. "Let's see how this would have worked."

Abdi pushed the rod into place, locking them between two plastered walls about fifteen inches apart, a space so narrow, they were forced to walk sideways.

"Where would this be inside the house, Nate Daniels?"

"I don't know," Nate said. "These must be the walls between two rooms."

Even with their flashlights, the light-eating darkness kept the visibility down to no more than a couple of feet on either side of them. Overhead, the low ceiling revealed exposed beams. Long plank boards like the kind in the alcove made up the floor, and the air around them was dry and stale.

After about twenty-five feet, Nate stopped as his right foot slid across the board and found nothing but air. He aimed the light to where the floor ended in a sharp drop. An old wooden ladder was wedged beneath the narrow gap. They needed to maneuver backward to climb down the rungs. Someone overweight would have a hard time doing this. Nate guessed people were smaller in the 1800's. Good thing he and Abdi were both skinny. He turned to Abdi.

"So, we go down?"

"We go down," Abdi agreed.

They descended into an alcove twice as long as the one at the bottom of the secret stairs. This was more like a small narrow hallway, approximately eight feet long by four feet wide and bare, except for the small desk and chair wedged under a slant in the ceiling.

"I think we might be under the front stairway," Nate said.

"I do not believe so. I remember the stairway being farther away."

"Yeah, you're right, but I think we're back on the first floor anyway. There's a pantry and a laundry room back-to-back. We could be in between them."

"Yes, where no one would notice the missing space."

"I'll check after I leave. I'll knock on the wall; knock back if you hear it. Maybe there's another way in."

"Yes, a second exit route would be useful."

Abdi still carried the apple and bananas, but he would need water and a blanket to sleep on.

"I should go get you some other stuff before my grandparents get back," Nate told him.

"I understand, but be careful. Take nothing for granted."

"I won't." He looked with wonder at Abdi, who had not been very big to begin with. How many miles had he biked in thirty-six hours to lose so much weight? Abdi looked at least fifteen pounds lighter than when Nate last saw him, and he didn't have fifteen pounds to lose. Maybe it was more than just the past two days. Maybe Abdi hadn't eaten since following them to the farm. He didn't look as though he had gotten much sleep either. The toll showed on every inch of the man. "I won't be long," Nate promised. He started up, then noticed the kerosene lamp on the desk. He aimed the flashlight at the yellow liquid still inside the flask.

"Do you think it still works?"

Abdi turned to the lantern. "We will see, if you can find matches."

"Done," Nate said, and hurriedly climbed up.

He walked to the laundry room where his grandparents kept extra pillows and blankets. He found bottled water in the pantry and also grabbed a toothbrush along with a box of matches. He piled everything on the kitchen table and then tried to guess Abdi's location inside the walls.

He stood before the china cupboard. They had gone up then moved sideways. He took twenty-five sideway steps to approximate the place on the landing where the passageway dropped off. That put him almost in front of his grandparents' bedroom so he entered. He and Abdi had gone down ten or twelve rungs on the ladder, so they hadn't gone farther than the first floor. Which wasn't the best situation because it meant Abdi was somewhere inside the walls of his grandparents' room and risked being heard when they were home.

A corner of the room had been made into a sitting area with a television. When he had watched *Secret of the Dead* here, he hadn't considered what the room might have been before his grandparents turned it into a bedroom. Maybe it had once been sleeping quarters for the help like a cook, a maid, or something. If Great-Gramps had lived here as a single man, that made sense. The room's huge size, along with a modern looking terrace beyond the French doors, suggested a remodel for sure. Most likely, this area had originally been divided into smaller rooms with a shared bath.

As in Mom's old room, the closet and bath were built side by side. A wider space separated the two doors, but each had the same dimensions.

The closet had been customized with shelves and racks mounted on opposite walls in his/her divide. If an exit from the hiding place was ever here, Nate doubted it still existed.

The bathroom had been updated too. It had a real shower and one of those sleek fountain type sinks. The one thing in his grandparents' remodeled bath that looked original and was not in his room or his mom's, was a linen closet. It was built into the wall shared with the clothes closet. *Did it work like the cupboard in the kitchen?*

He opened the linen closet and found shelves filled with toiletries and towels. He emptied the shelves then lifted them off the thin wooden slits that held them in place. He accidentally bumped a shelf against the wall while removing it. The bump must have sounded like a knock because Abdi's answering knock came. *So far, so good.*

Once the closet was bare, Nate methodically pulled and turned each wood bracket until the middle one shifted vertically. Without further nudging, the bracket glided along the back wall of its own accord. It reached the corner then dropped slowly along the edge. A ghostly hand seemed to guide it until Nate realized that a seam running across the wood must act like tracks. Peering closely, he saw the long, thin length of metal built into the grove like tiny railroad tracks. The middle bracket had been designed to run along it.

When the bracket finished its descent, a faint click came like a releasing latch. Great-Gramps really was ingenious.

Nate pushed the back walls of the linen closet. Nothing happened, *duh*. That would just lead to the clothes closet. He pushed the corner where the two tracks intercepted between the shared wall of the bath and clothes closet. He understood now why the wall between the bath and clothes closet was wider. Anyone would figure that the linen closet accounted for the larger space, but that was another decoy.

Nate felt the wall give a little, but layers of paint held it in place. He pushed harder until the outline of a small door cracked open. A bit more, and a door of maybe eighteen inches wide and twice as long swung open. Behind it, Abdi kneeled on the floor a few feet away.

"Okay, wait here." Nate grinned and hurried to the kitchen for the supplies. He returned and handed them to Abdi through the narrow opening.

"We need a signal so you'll know when the overhead door needs to be bolted. I'm going to have to bring you food through there, so you can't keep it locked. We can't use this entrance unless it's an emergency because you're between the walls of my grandparents' bathroom and closet."

"I understand," Abdi said. He looked like he would drop off to sleep at any moment. Maybe more planning could wait.

"Okay, I'll try to check back in later, but you should probably get some rest."

"Agreed," Abdi said then placed a hand over Nate's. "Thank you, Nate Daniels."

"Sure," Nate said and closed the opening. He returned the middle bracket to its home position, and then stood to put everything back inside the linen closet.

His mind swirled from things happening so fast. He stopped in the middle of placing some towels on a shelf as a revelation hit him.

Great-Gramps's antics with the picture frame had been trying to tell them how to find this place. Up-side-down was how to open the entrance from the linen closet. The wood bracket goes up, slides sideways, then drops down. It was also directions on how to find the hideaway. He and Abdi had walked up the stairs, sideways along the passage, then down the ladder. Still, if Great-Gramps had been at this for years, as his grandparents said, then Nathan Freedman had reasons for wanting the hiding place found, and it had nothing to do with helping Abdi.

# 20
# SEARCHED

Grandma and Granddad arrived home a few minutes after he settled Abdi into the hideaway. Nate told them about his mom's call, but not about the agents who searched the woods. He hadn't even told them about Abdi's car hidden there. He couldn't say why, but somehow he thought the less his grandparents knew, the less likely they would be held responsible if anything went wrong, if say, he and Abdi were convicted of plotting against the United States government.

He didn't worry as much for himself. At fifteen, and a new fifteen at that, the system might not be too hard on him. Abdi was young too, probably no more than ten years his senior. Hopefully, they wouldn't end up in Guantanamo Bay, the federal detention center he'd heard about on the news. His stomach flopped at the thought. His plan had to work but already he had problems.

When Grandma tried to return Mom's call in the afternoon, she couldn't get through the busy signal. Then later, he tried to call Hannah and Will to tell them about the note but got the same busy tone. He didn't tell his grandparents, but he suspected their phone line was being jammed. He would bet they weren't the only people with phone problems. Agents were probably blocking all communications on the mountain because they believed Abdi was still here. They didn't want him calling for help.

Without a way to communicate to anyone in the outside world, the farm felt more isolated than before. How had people once lived this way all the time?

Granddad planned to drive into town first thing in the morning to report the problem, but Nate didn't hold out much hope the problem would be resolved.

Both Grandma and Granddad seemed as anxious about not having phone service as he. He overheard them in the kitchen talking when he came down to say goodnight. They were discussing a disruption in some kind of *relay*, but when he entered, they changed the subject. Strange, they seriously seemed to have a lot of secrets for an elderly couple.

When he arrived at the farm five days ago, he never imagined being impatient for church. Now, it was the only way to clue the twins in on his plan. This was probably why church had played such an important role in the community before people had good stuff like cell phones, Facebook, and Twitter. Church had once been the fastest way to communicate a plan and galvanize support. Now, he needed to rely on the old-school method.

****

Wednesday morning finally dawned, and he got lucky because Grandma decided to ride into town with Granddad, giving Nate a chance to give Abdi breakfast.

Nate locked all the doors and closed the blinds before going to the kitchen and preparing a tray of food. This morning's breakfast included Grandma's blueberry muffins and a side of veggie sausages. He poured a glass of orange juice but then questioned his ability to deliver the juice unspilled. He grabbed two cans of soda instead. After more thought, he decided not to try and navigate through the narrow passage of the hideaway with the tray at all. The linen closet entrance in the bathroom would work better. He had told Abdi they should use it only in emergencies, but this was sort of like an emergency. Abdi had to eat.

After he emptied the linen closet, he turned the wood bracket that opened the entrance and let it run the tracks. He pushed open the concealed door. Abdi was kneeling a few feet away, busy chanting something.

Nate cleared his throat and Abdi looked his way.

"What are you doing?" he asked.

"Fajr is the Muslim morning prayer."

"I actually know that," Nate told him, "but it's way after dawn."

Abdi appeared disappointed. "My watch is broken. It is difficult to know the time."

"Yeah, it'd be impossible in this place." He wondered how long a runaway slave had had to stay in closed quarters like this, and how had they kept from going bonkers while doing so. "I'll see if I can find you something to tell time with before I leave." He pushed the tray forward, and Abdi reached over and took it.

Nate crawled through the narrow gap and then sat cross-legged on the floor with Abdi.

"How is it that you know of Muslim prayer?" Abdi asked as he took a big bite of muffin.

"Our church back home has a faith-based community exchange program," Nate told him. "You have to live with people of another faith during their holiday celebration. My parents signed me up for the exchange when I was twelve."

"And what did you learn about the Muslim faith?"

"They pray a lot," Nate answered.

Abdi smiled. "Indeed we do."

He debated telling Abdi about the phone line. On the one hand, Abdi couldn't really do anything about it, and the news would just worry him more. On the other hand, Abdi was the spy here. Maybe he knew a way around this obstacle.

"The phone line is down," Nate blurted.

Abdi looked instinctively around the room as though checking for a window. "Has there been a storm?"

"No storm," Nate said. "Our calls just won't go through."

"Then they are most likely tampering with phone communication. We must bide our time and you must avoid doing anything to bring attention to yourself."

"But the phone lines are *down*," Nate said with more force. "How long can they block calls?"

"Exactly," Abdi said. "There are time limits to this line of action. A prolonged disruption of communications will endanger the community. They cannot continue for very much longer. They must hurry to set up monitoring devices."

"You mean taps on our phones?" Nate asked. "Is that still legal?"

"It is legal, Nate Daniels."

"So even when we get phone service back, we need to watch what we say?"

"Even with no telephone monitoring, Nate Daniels, you must watch what you say."

"Don't worry," Nate assured him. "I'll be careful. Hold on, I'll be right back." He squeezed through the gap once more and darted upstairs to his room. He grabbed the alarm clock on the nightstand then hurried down again. He handed the clock to Abdi through the hideaway door. "Take this to help with your prayers," he said.

Abdi looked at the electric cord dangling on the end of the clock.

"It has a battery back-up," Nate told him.

Abdi bowed. Nate thought he did that a lot. He bowed back and was backing out of the closet when the doorbell rang. He froze as panic shot through him.

Abdi's face clouded with deep concern. He set the tray on the floor and moved to push the door closed. "You must hurry, Nate Daniels," he said before the gap disappeared and Nate heard the latch engage.

Shaking and near frantic, Nate returned the shelves to the linen closet and hurriedly shoved the towels and toiletries inside. He wasn't sure how long restocking the closet had taken, but the doorbell rang three more times while he hurried to hide the entrance.

He walked to the front foyer, as jumpy as a jackrabbit with too much caffeine. Through the long narrow side window of the door, the shoulder of someone wearing a black suit was visible. In the driveway beyond the shoulder, a black Mercedes was parked. He relaxed. *Only Reverend Ellis.*

He opened the door and immediately tensed again.

"Federal agents." The man flashed a badge. "Where are your parents, son?"

"In Boston," Nate answered.

"You're here alone?" the agent questioned.

"Yeah," Nate said.

The man studied him suspiciously. "You live here alone?"

"No," Nate told him. "I'm staying with my grandparents for the summer."

The agent wore dark sunshades, but Nate could feel his eyes roll. "You might have said that to begin with, kid."

*You might have asked,* Nate thought. "Can I help you?"

"Ask your grandparents to come to the door. We need to instigate a search of the premises."

"My grandparents went into town." Nate didn't recognize his voice for the pounding drum roll in his ears. *A search!* "I'm alone here."

"Then step outside, son." The agent nodded to more men waiting in the driveway. Nate hadn't seen their line of cars through the window. Half a dozen government vehicles parked in single file. Now a wall of agents was moving toward the house.

# 21
# INFILTRATED

"I don't think my grandparents would allow a search of their home. You should probably come back when they're here," Nate said, closing the door.

The agent grabbed the edge and pushed it open again. "We don't need their permission, son. We have a Special Executive Order. Now, step out of the house," the agent said as if he was talking to someone with a limited intellect.

Fearing that too much protest would draw the agent's suspicion, Nate stepped onto the porch. Another agent took him by the arm and walked him down the steps. The agent opened a door to one of the cars when they reached the driveway. He pushed Nate's head down as he guided him inside the government-issue vehicle and then turned and went back to the house.

Nate watched him go up the steps and through the door guarded by two agents standing on either side of the entrance. All the other agents must have already gone inside. In all, there were about a dozen of them.

Nate couldn't be sure, but the agents at the door seemed to watch him. He needed to act normal. But what was normal in a situation like this? Should he cooperate or be offended? Should he look relieved or scared? He couldn't decide. He turned his gaze to the meadows where patches of fog still lingered and morning dew looked like frost on the green blades of grass. Mist floating slowly in the distance reminded him of spirits. *Now is a good time to blow gusts of wind and upturn pictures, Great-Gramps.* Anything to scare them out of the house.

Great-Gramps had been a genius, just as Hannah said. Years had gone by and no one had stumbled onto the house's secret. This might have given Nate comfort, except no one had been looking for a concealed space. These guys were some of America's finest. If he could find the stairway, then they could too. Once inside, they only needed to accidentally step on the right board to release the floor latch, and Abdi would be doomed. He hoped Abdi had remembered the metal rod on the hideaway door and had put the lock in place.

A hum from an engine sounded behind him. He tensed as he thought about his grandparents returning from town and twisted around on the seat. It wasn't a silver Lincoln, but another black Mercedes coming toward the house.

The car pulled up to the walkway, and the rear door swung open even before the car came to a complete stop. A giant of a man stepped out. He looked to be over six-foot-five and wore tons of medals on his green uniform jacket. The other riders, three stuffy looking bureaucrats in fatigues, had waited for the driver to stop before joining the giant on the walk.

The giant's eyes, almost lost under thick bushy black brows peppered with white, darted past the half-dozen vehicles parked along the driveway and then to the house. "Who's in charge here?" he commanded to no one in particular. One of the men guarding the door marched down the steps like a tin soldier and gave a report.

"Special Agent Beckman is inside leading the search, sir."

"Get him out here," the giant ordered.

"Yes, sir," the guard said and ran back up the steps and into the house.

A few moments later, a man in a black tailored suit walked outside. He moved briskly down the walkway and gave a clipped nod to the giant. Nate didn't recognize him as the man who knocked at the door earlier. He must have blended in with the other agents when they entered the house.

The giant gave the man, who Nate assumed was Special Agent Beckman, a piercing look. "Why has this sole terrorist not been apprehended, Beckman?" the giant said in a way that sounded like an insult to the agent's competence, but the agent answered as if he hadn't heard the implication.

"Sir, I have men covering all known points of exits from the area. We feel sure the terrorist is using the woods to avoid capture. However, he has no resources. It is only a matter of time before he's captured or dead."

"Then why the hell aren't you people combing the woods? What in damnation are you doing here?"

"Sir," Special Agent Beckman said, "my people are scouting the woods as well as conducting a door-to-door search of every house on the mountain in case the subject has taken cover in or near a resident's home."

This piqued the giant's interest. "You seriously think this fugitive is being aided by a civilian?"

"Perhaps not willingly, sir, or even knowingly. We're conducting a house to house search to ensure we leave no stone unturned."

It seemed to Nate some of the thunder went out of the giant as he considered what the agent had said. When he spoke, it was slow and deliberate. "You must make it clear to all the residents here that aiding this terrorist will be considered an act of treason. Anyone doing so will be prosecuted to the full extent of the law."

"Yes, sir," the agent said, seeming somewhat taken aback. "To be clear, sir, we don't believe the terrorist is being deliberately aided by residents. He may have taken shelter in a shed, or one of the many hunting stations constructed in this part of the country."

The giant considered this. "Have you questioned any of the residents, Special Agent Beckman?"

Once again, the agent looked surprised by the question. "No sir, we have no reason to interrogate these people, only to make them aware they need to be alert in this situation."

"I would like you to question them as well, Special Agent Beckman. Make sure they're aware that the man we're looking for can be persuasive at twisting the truth and may even gain a certain degree of sympathy."

"Of course, sir," the agent said, still looking puzzled.

"I would like to speak to the people of this house myself."

"Begging your pardon, sir, may I ask why?"

"The terrorist's rental car was located on this property, am I correct?"

"Yes, sir," the agent answered.

"Then I'd like a word with the owners, Special Agent Beckman."

"Yes sir. But the car was found in the woods over a mile away from this location."

"Nevertheless, I would like to speak with these people."

"Yes, sir. As I understand it, the owners of the property went into town. There's only a teenage kid here. He's waiting in one of the cars while we conduct the search." The agent pointed to the Mercedes where Nate sat.

"Bring him to me," the giant command.

"Sir, I believe he's a minor. We'll need permission from a guardian ..."

"Beckman," the giant's voice boomed then dropped to a controlled level. "Bring me the boy." Nate's heart doubled in size and beat wildly in his chest. He struggled to get his breath and control the panic threatening to erupt. They wanted to question him.

# 22
## INTERROGATED

Special Agent Beckman made a choppy hand movement, and one of the agents guarding the porch rushed down the steps and opened the car door. "Come on, kid." He grabbed Nate's arm and pulled him from the car.

"What's going on?" Nate tried to sound innocent.

"It'll be okay," the agent said under his breath so that Nate barely heard. Gripping Nate's arm, the guard guided him over to the giant and Special Agent Beckman.

"What's your name, son?" Special Agent Beckman asked.

"Nate Daniels," he said. "Is something wrong?" He didn't know how far to push this innocent routine. After all, he would be an idiot not to know about the manhunt by now. Still, as a kid, how much would he care?

"Nate, I'm Special Agent Joshua Beckman with Homeland Security." The agent shook Nate's hand. "And this is General Jalapa." Nate looked at the general whose severe expression told him the man wasn't used to dealing with people socially. The heavy stanch of cigarettes clung to the man like an invisible cloak. "Nate, the general would like to ask you a few questions if it's okay with you."

"About what?" Nate asked.

"We'll get to that," General Jalapa said abruptly. "Special Agent, I require someplace for interrogation."

"We can use one of the rooms inside the house, sir."

"Lead the way," the general ordered.

General Jalapa, Special Agent Beckman, and Nate entered the library. Nate was told to sit on a couch while General Jalapa and the agent each took a wing chair facing him and the mountains.

Nate must have looked as tense as he felt because the agent smiled and said, "Relax. This won't take long." He winked at Nate.

"But I don't know anything," Nate said.

"But you might," General Jalapa said sharply. "You may have seen something without realizing it. Have you noticed anything out of the ordinary over the last few days?" The general squinted beneath his mega brow. "It was Nate, correct?"

"Not really, I mean, yes, my name is Nate, but I haven't seen anything out of the ordinary."

"It might have been something small. Something you didn't give much thought to at the time," General Jalapa said. "Perhaps something went missing or you found something misplaced."

"No, sir," Nate said. "Nothing like that."

"I see. Do you consider yourself familiar with these woods?"

"No, sir. I'm a noob ... I mean; I just got here last Saturday. I haven't had a lot of chances to go exploring."

"You arrived here on Saturday?" The general's interest piqued once more. Too late, Nate realized he had given too much away.

"Well, yes, sir. I'm visiting my grandparents for the summer. So I don't really know much about this area."

"Where are you from, boy?"

"Boston."

"And you arrived on Saturday, you say?"

"Yes, sir. Like I said, I'm just visiting my grandparents for the summer."

"Special Agent." The general turned to Beckman. "That's the day we searched the plane from Boston at the Charlotte airport, correct?"

"Yes, sir. Before we learned of the second terrorist. We were hoping to capture Conwell, but he must've gotten suspicious and changed the plan." The agent reached inside his suit jacket and pulled out a small black notebook. He flipped the pages then read an entry aloud. "Flight 417 out of Boston, sir."

"Special Agent Beckman, get me a list of passengers from that flight."

"Yes, sir." The agent stood and left Nate alone with Mr. Congeniality.

"Do you remember what flight you flew down on, boy?" Nate wondered why the general had even bothered to ask his name if he was going to keep calling him boy.

"I don't remember, sir. I have a bad memory for stuff like that."

"But you're from Boston, you say?"

"Yes, sir."

"What kind of work do your parents do?"

"My dad works in computer technology and my mom's an accountant."

"Computer technology? Is that for the government or the private sector?"

"Private sector, sir."

"We're going to need your parents names, son."

*Right, you start calling me son, and I'm supposed to tell you anything you want to know. Not happening.*

"I don't think I should say anymore until my grandparents get back." Nate congratulated himself on that one. Make the general think he's trying to cover something up about his parents, thereby launching a useless investigation into his parents while deflecting attention from Abdi. *I'm good at this spy stuff.*

"Are you saying you don't want to help find an enemy of your country?"

"No, sir. I'm not saying that. I want to help my country in any way I can."

"Good, then you won't mind cooperating with our investigation?"

"Well, no. I don't mind." *Okay, point to the general.*

Special Agent Beckman came back waving a sheet of paper. He gave Nate a quizzical look before handing the paper to Godzilla-Brow. "The list of passengers, sir."

The general scanned the page. "Nathanial Daniels from Boston. That would be you, boy."

"Yes, sir."

"And you didn't remember your plane had been delayed and searched?"

Nate opened and closed his mouth, looking speechless, which didn't require too much acting. "Wow, is that what that was about? I didn't make the connection. I mean, I was just glad to be done with it. I guess I just didn't think anything more about it."

"It seems more than coincidental for two passengers with no connection to end up in the same remote location."

"Uh, I don't know what you mean."

"There was a passenger using the name of Maher Serboa who flew down on the plane with you. His rental car was found abandoned just over a mile from this location."

"Oh, then yes, sir," Nate said. "That's freaky."

The general leaned forward in his chair. "The man we're looking for is highly intelligent. He has managed to breach high-level security files and copied military documents he plans to use to aid terrorists in attacks against American soldiers. It is vital we capture him before he can deliver those files." The general leaned back but looked no less intimidating. "We know he has an accomplice who's still at large, and that he plans to deliver the information he stole within the next forty-eight hours." The general looked at Nate as if he was trying to read his soul. "If you remember anything, no matter how small, you must contact us immediately. Do you understand?"

The general's argument was persuasive. Anyone listening to him would be inspired to do his or her civic duty. And if he delivered that same spiel to everyone around here, Nate was going to have a much harder time getting Abdi out of the mountains.

"Absolutely, sir."

Just then, a gust of wind blew into the room and the temperature dropped about thirty degrees.

"What is that?" General Jalapa asked, darting his beady gaze around the room, looking about for the source of the cold draft as if it was a living entity.

"What is what, sir?" Special Agent Beckman, seated in a chair again, scanned the room to see what the general was referring to. The general eyed him irritably.

"The damn chill, man. Can't you feel it?"

Beckman shook his head. "I'm fine, sir."

"Dammit, Beckman, find out where that blast is coming from!"

The agent stood, looking completely baffled. "Yes, sir," he said and did a check of the windows in the room. "Sir, the windows are secure."

"Then check something else, Beckman. Kill that damn wind."

Special Agent Beckman looked at Nate. "Where's the AC control?" he asked.

"Oh, uh, it's in the dining room. I can show you." Nate stood, feeling the presence of the ghost too, but obviously not as much as the general who started to shiver and stood to walk back and forth on the rug in front of his chair. What puzzled Nate was why Special Agent Beckman didn't feel it at all. Nate led him to the thermostat, which read a comfy seventy-three degrees.

"The AC is programmed to turn on once the temperature passes seventy-five," Nate explained. "No air is blowing right now."

"Do you feel any draft?" the agent asked.

Nate shrugged. "I don't know what he's talking about," Nate lied. He'd already figured out the unexplained gusts and breezes. Great-Gramps communicated his moods this way. The old spirit sent warm breezes when he was happy, but a cold breeze signaled frustration or anger. But what Nathan Freedman the First was saying about General Jalapa, Nate had no clue.

# 23
# CHURCH

The situation had become dire. Now getting Abdi safely off the mountain meant Nate had to do so under the noses of federal agents.

At least everything had returned to *looking* normal before his grandparents got home. General Jalapa hadn't recovered from his bout with the chills; in fact, he had started to turn blue before deciding he must be getting sick and left. The temperature returned to normal the moment he did.

While searching for General Jalapa's draft, which remained a mystery, the agents finished their search of the house. Amazingly, the secret stairway had not been found. Nate had waited half an hour after watching them leave before daring to use the secret stairway to go see Abdi. Just thinking of the chance that agents would return while he was still in the hideaway caused a fist-sized knot to grow in his stomach. He couldn't remember ever feeling so scared.

He told Abdi all that happened as quickly as he could. Abdi only nodded and listened, looking extremely intense.

"And they're searching for someone named Maher Serboa," Nate's voice was low, breathless with the kind of excitement that came with fear. "Is that the name of your partner?"

"No, it is one of my aliases. I have others."

Nate studied him a moment. "Is Abdi even your real name?"

"On my honor, it is. However, we must devise a signal, no? A way to say the coast is clear."

"I've been thinking about that," Nate said. "If I knock four times, that'll mean everything is okay. You knock two times to let me know you heard."

Abdi nodded. "And what if the coast is not clear?"

"We'll reverse it. I'll give two knocks and you answer with four."

"Very well, Nate Daniels. Remember, you must be very careful."

Nate turned and hurried up the ladder then looked back. "Nathan Freedman's ghost blew cold air at General Jalapa. I think it means something."

"Your ancestor has proven to be very wise," Abdi said. "Be especially careful of this General Jalapa."

****

Nate stood with Hannah and Will in the church's entry hall.

"We've been trying to reach you," Hannah announced the moment Grandma and Granddad left them alone. She slipped her arm inside Nate's as they followed the flow of people into the sanctuary. "Is something wrong with your phone?" she asked, sounding exasperated.

Wednesday evening Bible Study had finally arrived. Nate, at last, had a chance to speak with Hannah and Will. He squeezed Hannah's hand but kept quiet as they moved through the unexpectedly heavy gathering in search of a quiet spot inside the church. Seems like news of a terrorist loose in the area brought people together.

"Everything's been crazy," Nate told them once they had settled in a pew at the very back. "Tons of stuff has been happening at the farm. Yesterday, agents found Abdi's car in the woods, and they came up to the house today."

"What did they do?" Will asked, sounding uneasy.

"They asked me questions about Abdi."

"What did you tell them?" Hannah said.

"I told them I didn't know anything. Like we agreed."

"Man, this is getting deep," Will said. "But they found the car themselves, and we really don't know much more than that, right?"

Nate changed the subject because he wasn't ready to tell them about Abdi or his plan. It wasn't something you could just lead with. He pulled a copy of the note he found in the mantel from his pocket. The real note was too fragile to carry around.

"I found something." Nate handed the note he copied to Will. He waited as Hannah and Will read it together.

"What is this?" Will asked.

"I copied this from an old piece of paper I found. I would have called you when I first found it, but it was three A.M."

"And you're thinking this has something to do with the Underground Railroad?" Will asked.

"Don't you? I think these are coded directions. I've been doing some research, and symbols and codes played a big part in the Railroad movement."

"You could be right. Peg-Leg Joe's song, '*Follow the Drinking Gourd*' basically told slaves how to follow the North Star to freedom and what signs to look for along the way." Will looked like he owned a You Tube video that just went viral. He grinned and asked, "So, you want to crack the code?"

"Uh, duh," Nate said. The three crowded together on the pew with Hannah in the middle and studied the copy.

When the North Wind blows

Find the falling snow

Seek out the gray snake

On its back lies the gate

Keep your eyes to the sky

As the moon passes by

The brightest light you'll see

Is the guide you must heed

Persevere and keep hope

Help lies upon the Northern slope

"I'd say we definitely got directions," Will said after they all read the note again.

"I agree." Hannah smiled and squeezed Nate's hand. "Where did you find this?"

"Inside a hole in one of the columns on the mantel in my room."

"What kind of hole?" Will asked.

"I don't know. Someone just dug out a hole long enough to stuff the note inside and then covered it with a wooden cap."

"And you just happened to be poking about the mantel?" Will asked.

"Well, the cap fell off and that's when I saw it." Nate thought this was close enough to the truth.

Hannah beamed. "You've done so well, Nathan."

"Yeah, you did okay," Will admitted. "But don't get your hopes up. Remember, most slaves couldn't read. So this note may have nothing to do with the Railroad."

"Yes," Hannah said, "but there were exceptions. Maybe this was meant for someone specific, someone who could read."

"We can argue the point later," Will said. "Let's try to work out what it means before someone figures out we're not back here studying the Bible. Let's go line-by-line and piece it together."

Hannah took the note from Will and then placed it on a page of her open Bible. By all appearances, it looked as though she was reading from the Scriptures.

"*When the North wind blows, find the falling snow,*" she read quietly.

"That's pretty obvious," Will said. "It means to head North in the winter."

"Yeah, that's what I think too," Nate said.

Hannah nodded and read the next line. "*Seek out the gray snake, on his back lies the gate.*"

"According to my research," Nate said, "the gray snake most likely meant the Ohio River. It would have been frozen in the winter. If you were a runaway slave who couldn't swim or catch a ferry, crossing the river during the winter was your best bet."

"Right," Will said. "You have to remember, topography wasn't like it is today. There weren't many ways to go north."

Hannah said, "We know most slaves running to freedom had to cross the Ohio River, so that makes sense." She looked down and read the next two lines, *"Keep your eyes to the sky, as the moon passes by."*

"Easy one," Nate said. "It means to travel by night." The twins both nodded and Hannah read again.

*"The brightest light you'll see is the guide you must heed."*

"That could be another reference to follow the North Star," Will said. "Or it could mean the burning lanterns station masters left out on the porch during the night. It signaled a safe house."

Hannah reached the last two lines. *"Persevere and keep hope. Help lies upon the Northern slopes."*

"That's the most puzzling line," Nate said. "What could it mean?"

"Given the circumstances," Hannah said, "I think it means the location of your grandparents' house. Northern slopes must have meant the mountains of North Carolina. This part was probably meant to tell runaways where to find a place of rest."

"Han is probably right. Your grandparents' place was probably more isolated back then than it is now. So any runaway seeing the tale-tale sign of a burning lantern on the porch would be drawn there. There was a code they used, 'A friend with friends.' But if we can locate a hiding place on your grandparents' farm, that would clinch this."

"I think it's already clinched," Hannah said. "It's obvious. The recipient of the note was to leave in winter, cross a frozen river, travel only by night using the North Star as a guide. The journey would have probably taken a long time; hence, the perseverance part and a promise of help. What other group of people in America would need such coded instructions? This is our proof."

"Well, actually," Nate said, grinning, "that's sort of the other half of my news." He lowered his voice to barely a whisper. "I found something that will clinch this."

"Found what?" Hannah whispered back.

"There's a hidden space inside the secret stairs."

"Get out!" Will said a bit too loud and caused several people to turn toward them with concerned stares. Will waved and smiled. "Sorry," he mouthed then turned back to Nate. "What? When?"

"Yesterday afternoon. And there's more. Abdi is hiding out there."

"Say what?" Will said with the smile gone from his face.

"Come again?" Hannah said, arching her brow.

"I know," Nate said. "But we have to help him get to the Pentagon. He showed up yesterday because he couldn't get through the road-blocks around the mountain. He won't make it without our help."

"Nathan, this is insane!"

"I know," Nate said. "That's what I said too."

"So, you just need us to talk some sense into you?" Will said.

Nate exhaled, racking his brain for a way to convince the twins that helping Abdi was the right thing to do. "Why don't you come to the house and talk to him. Judge for yourself if he's someone capable of committing a terrorist act."

"Well, I think we should," Hannah said then gasped. "Nathan! He was in the house all night while you and your grandparents slept? Wait!" Hannah caught her breath sharply and put a hand to her chest. "Do your grandparents know? They're in on this?"

"No!" It was Nate turn to crunch his face. "They're grandparents. They wouldn't do anything like that."

"Wrong," Hannah told him. "They take risks all the time. You heard them talk about the reverend's packages for delivery, haven't you?"

"I heard them mention picking up a package for the reverend. Didn't make much sense."

"Well, it does if you understand that 'package' is Reverend Ellis's code word for distressed soul."

"Yeah," Will said. "Seems like our grandparents are running a little underground operation of their own. It's mostly abused women and their children running away from violent husbands to start a new life."

"Yes," Hannah said. "It's supposed to be hush-hush, but we found out about it yesterday when your grandparents picked up a 'package' but couldn't deliver it."

"Too many stop points and checks," Will added. "I guess normally, no one suspects a sweet elderly couple of smuggling people across state lines. That's why Reverend Ellis likes to use the older members of his congregation."

"But," Nate said, "why do you say smuggle? They're just helping people, right?"

"Not exactly," Hannah explained. "The fathers have a legal right to their kids. A mother cannot run off and start a new life without the father's permission. Of course, he's unlikely to give permission. And if he knew where they were, he would hunt them down and the cycle of violence would start again."

"So what they're doing is illegal," Will said. "Your grandparents couldn't get their package to a safe house yesterday, so they went off the cuff. There's this rule the package is never to stay in the same place twice while they're on the run. It's one of the safeguards. So the mom and her three kids spent the night in our grandparents' basement because they couldn't go back to the church. Your grandparents were afraid they couldn't get them past all the roadblocks because everyone was required to show ID. Since the runaways don't get new IDs until after they reach the safe house, the package delivery got canned."

"Wow," Nate said, seeing his chance to use the information as leverage. "Our grandparents risk jail time to help do the right thing. Shouldn't we follow their example? Abdi needs our help. And if we help him, we'll be helping to protect our troops and maybe the nation."

"I don't know, Nathan. The government is telling everyone to turn him in; they're saying *he is* a terrorist."

"Yeah, I know, but sometimes our government is wrong." He watched Hannah's and Will's gazes fall to the note, maybe thinking about another time when the nation had stood on the wrong side of right.

"All right," Hannah finally said. "We agree to talk to him, but that is all we can promise."

# 24
# THE PLAN

Nate and his grandparents were back on the farm by nine. Grandma heated the dinner she had made earlier but no one had had a chance to eat during their crazy day. Nate pretended he didn't feel well and asked to take a tray to his room. After checking his forehead for a fever and forcing him to take a spoonful of some nasty tasting stuff called Castor oil, his grandma gave him a tray and sent him upstairs.

Nate took the tray to the hideaway. He balanced the tray by pressing it against the side of his hipbone with one arm as he squeezed along the narrow corridor until he reached the ladder. Abdi must have heard him coming because he was waiting at the bottom of the ladder and took the tray so that Nate could climb down.

"Sorry it took so long to get you more food," Nate said as he hopped down the last few rungs in the dim alcove. He hadn't brought Abdi anything to eat since breakfast. This bothered him because Abdi couldn't afford to lose any more weight, and he was going to need all his strength to pull off the plan.

To Nate's surprise, Abdi placed the tray against the back wall of the desk, even though he had to be starving. Abdi picked up an old looking journal lying open on the desk. "Please sit," Abdi told him, nodding to the chair. "I would like to read you something." Abdi took the kerosene lamp burning on the desk and placed it on the floor then sat crossed-leg before it. Nate didn't take the chair but joined Abdi on the floor because it felt more like they were at a campfire.

"Listen," Abdi said, meeting Nate's eyes. "Listen," he said again the way teachers do to show they really mean it. He read:

*March 2, 1857*

*There is a Negro man hiding in the woods behind the farm. He has been there for days, foraging on berries and nuts from the trees. We leave food out at night, but he does not approach the house. I wonder about him as he must wonder about my household and me. Are we friends or are we foes?*

*March 8, 1857*

*After over a week, Benjamin has decided we are sympathizers and has given us his trust for the safe completion of his journey. I find it strange that he did not judged me by the color of my skin. For who would turn in a kinsman? Yet, to be judged completely on one's character is a refreshing change.*

*March 15th, 1857*

*Today we forwarded bales of cotton to Kentucky. Benjamin was bounded into a loosely packed bale with only small holes to allow for the insertion of narrow stems of dried cattails through which to draw air. With Mr. Duncan's help, the cotton will be loaded onto a riverboat. We trust God's good will to deliver him to the next station master and the next conductor, until he is finally free.*

Abdi finished and looked at him. "You are a descendant of a brave and noble man, Nate Daniels. It is in your blood, yes?"

Nate could barely believe what he just heard. Abdi held the proof he needed. "A journal? Where … How did you find it?"

Abdi nodded to the desk. "There are letters in the drawer as well." He reached past the lantern and offered Nate the journal with his head bowed.

Nate took it and ran a hand across the worn brown leather surface with layers of dust caked in hundreds of tiny cracks. Some of the faded gold initials embossed in the center had flaked off, but Nate could still make out the letters **NF**. He held Nathan Freedman's records.

"Man, Abdi, I was hoping to find something like this. Thank you."
Abdi bowed again. "You would have found it, but I am glad to be of assistance."

Nate looked up from the journal and shook his head. "No, I don't think I would have found this if it wasn't for you. I wouldn't have found this hiding place or this journal if you hadn't come back."

"Then I think our paths were meant to cross, yes?"

"Yes," Nate agreed, smiling and holding the journal against his chest. "But we need to talk about how to get you out of here. I have a plan, but I'm going to need some help."

"I do not believe it is wise to tell anyone I am here, Nate Daniels."

"Yeah, too late. They're coming by to meet you tomorrow."

Concern reflected off Abdi's face with an intense focus. "What is your plan?"

\*\*\*\*

Hannah and Will arrived the next morning at ten as planned. This time a girl cousin named Cookie dropped them off. Nate told his grandparents they needed to finish sorting through the books in his room then led the twins upstairs.

They continued to his mom's old room and down the secret stairs. When they reached the middle landing, they stopped.

"Okay, you have to promise to give him a chance. Don't go in there with any attitude and preconceived ideas," Nate told them.

"For crying out loud. Just open the entrance," Will said.

"I'm just saying ..."

"Nathan," Hannah interrupted. "We are nervous enough. Please, let's get on with it."

"Okay." Nate gave up. "It's narrow, so I'll go first, then Will, then you, Hannah. Ready?"

"Ready, already," Will said.

Nate found the pressure point on the floorboard and leaned his weight into it. The wall cracked and he pushed it open wider and stepped inside. The twins followed, looking intimidated and keeping quiet.

With his back against the wall, Nate leaned forward and aimed a small flashlight from his pocket at the door. "Can you push the opening close and shove that metal bar in place to lock it?" he asked Hannah.

"Got it," Hannah said. Once she finished, she kept her hands up as if she was being taken hostage.

"Relax, he won't bite," Nate said. "It's just a few feet ahead."

They sidestepped along the floor to the ladder then climbed down. Abdi rose from the desk when he saw them. He stepped forward and waited with his hands cupped in front of him.

"Hey," Nate said as he they reached the alcove. He pulled a candy bar from his pocket and handed it to Abdi. "My grandparents are still in the kitchen. I'll get you breakfast as soon as they find something to do."

"Thank you, Nate Daniels." Abdi looked silently at the twins, who fidgeted. Will shifted from foot to foot while Hannah swayed slightly in place.

"Abdi Ahmead," Nate said, "these are my friends, Hannah and Will Greathouse. They're going to help us."

Abdi bowed. "I am in your debt."

"Well," Hannah started hesitantly, "we would like to ask you some questions first."

Abdi nodded then waited for her to continue.

"Okay." Hannah cleared her throat. "Great." She walked over and took a seat at the desk. "Mr. Ahmead, I have a computer." Hannah pulled a seven-inch notebook computer from her purse and then opened it. "Do you have any objection to us having a look at that USB?"

Abdi took the device from his pocket and bowed again as he handed it to her.

"Thank you." Hannah took the USB timidly. She plugged it into a port on the computer and everyone formed a semicircle around her.

Even though Nate decided to trust Abdi days ago, he still felt relieved when the computer screen displayed the content of the USB and no photographs of secret files or documents popped up. The USB was a video recording of a military base somewhere that looked like Mount Everest. Patches of snow spotted the dark gray ground and harsh outcropping of rocks overlooked mountains.

It seemed at first to be a harmless recording of the daily lives of soldiers on base, going about their business. But as the film continued, it became clear the film had an ulterior motive. This wasn't just bits and pieces of *a day in the life* … This was a full documentary of the platoon's routine. Someone watching the film could learn their schedule for everyday of the week, including times they slept and ate. The USB would give enemies information about when the platoon was the most vulnerable for an attack.

Judging by how casual the other soldiers treated him, whoever recorded the video had to be someone on base. There was no way to know if the filmmaker was Special Ops or a SAS agent. Either way, they were watching an act of treason.

"How did you get this, Abdi?" Nate asked.

"The soldier filming is a Taliban spy. I was his contact. The information on this USB is the last piece of information needed in order to ambush the installation."

"But who is filming?"

"I never saw his face. I left instructions for him in a particular location, and he delivered the information in the same manner. I do not know who he is, but I have his fingerprints off the device. When we discover his identity, we can use this information to reveal the mole at the Pentagon who planted him there."

"What about his voice?" Nate asked. "Did he have an accent?" If the traitor had an accent, then it wasn't a member of the Special Ops unit the twins loved so much. But when he thought about it, an accent wouldn't really mean anything. Americans had accents on top of accents. Many of his neighbors back in Boston had accents, including Ell's mom.

"We never spoke," Abdi explained. "We communicated by leaving signs or notes for each to follow."

An American terrorist didn't sit right with Nate, nor did the betrayal of an ally nation. This was messed up. He hoped they had time to fix it.

Hannah asked, "Abdi, why did they let you leave with this?"

"They did not. I was nearly killed during my escape. My contact here in the States planned to deliver the USB to the Pentagon at great risk to himself. I do not know if he is still alive."

"I'm sorry," Hannah said. "You must be worried about your friend. You're very brave. This USB is the proof the military needs to take action, but how will it prove you're an undercover operative?"

"Alone, the USB is not enough proof. Before we infiltrated the Taliban's camp, we were given a code word to speak to a certain general at the Pentagon. When he sees this USB and hears my word, he will know who I am."

"Wait," Will said, "that can't be all."

"There is one other thing I cannot reveal. You must now make a leap of faith."

****

Will and Hannah were on-board. That left one last person to persuade. The whole plan hinged on this person's cooperation.

Phone service returned twenty hours after going down, just as Abdi predicted. Nate would never take the phone for granted again. So much could depend on a phone call, like the one he was about to make.

After his call was answered, Nate was engaged in conversation that he guessed was Southern hospitality. He was asked about his health, his grandparents' health, and about how the farm was treating him. Finally, Billy's mom called him to the phone.

Nate asked Billy if they could meet at the crash point and hoped Billy wouldn't say something to force him to be more specific. He was 100 percent sure the phones were bugged. But Billy picked up on his meaning right away and hung up without asking for any explanation.

An hour later, Nate waited by the downed log Billy had crashed into two days earlier. He jumped when the kid leaped from behind a maple.

"I gotcha good," Billy said then grinned.

"That wasn't cool," Nate said sternly.

"Yeah, it was," Billy said, walking over then taking a seat on the log beside him. "You ready for your lesson?"

"Not today. I need a favor, and I need you not to tell anybody about the favor. Can you do that?"

"A favor? So, that means you gonna owe me?"

"Big time, Billy."

"So, what's the favor?"

# 25
# ESCAPE AT 10 P.M.

Nate, the twins, and Abdi huddled together in the hideaway. Hours earlier the twins returned to the farm, reporting success. They had convinced Reverend Ellis a distressed soul was in desperate need of emergency transportation, but the reverend hesitated to lend a car because of their age. The twins promised someone of legal age would drive. Plus, they promised to return the car safely and offered Will as an additional member of his congregation on Sundays for an entire month. The reverend finally agreed.

With the help of more of the twins' cousins, two cars had been driven to a designated location, but only one was driven back. A car now waited in a spot across the Tennessee border that Google Maps claimed was isolated except for a couple of houses and a general store.

"Okay," Nate said, "agents will be monitoring Abdi's rental, so when I drive off with it, they'll come after me. Except I'm not sure they'll turn on any sirens, so your cue will be when I honk the horn three times. It's important you wait for my signal before you move. Go too soon and you may be spotted."

The twins nodded and he continued. "When you hear the horn, you get Abdi to the crash spot I showed you. Billy marked the path with reflective duct tape on the north and south side of the trees running up the mountain." He looked at each twin. "Remember, pull the south side tape off as you pass. If for some reason you have to come back here, use the north side tape to find your way, understand?"

"We got it," Will said.

"Once you reach the crash point, keep using the duct tape markings to make your way to the top of the mountain. Once at the top, take the path on the right for about a mile. Billy left his ATV there with the keys in the ignition." He looked at Abdi. "Billy says the path is pretty well worn. That's why he and his brother don't like it, not much of a challenge. But that's good for you. Just stay on the path and don't go too fast. It crosses over to the Tennessee border some thirty miles from there."

"I understand," Abdi said then turned to Will and Hannah. "Tell me again where to find the car."

"It's near a billboard advertising a 7-Eleven. There's a mile marker, number four. A sign says it's a rest stop, but it's only a pull-off area with a cement picnic table. The car is parked there." Hannah opened her purse and took out a key. She gave it to Abdi. "The car is a white two-door; you shouldn't have trouble finding it."

Abdi took the keys and nodded then turned to Nate. "Are you sure you want to do your part, Nate Daniels? There is potential of great risk."

"No biggie, I'm a good driver." He smiled wide and shrugged.

"But how can you be certain they won't shoot you?" Hannah asked.

"They'll think I'm Abdi. They don't want him dead. They're going to want to question him."

"You're guessing about that," Will said. "Look, when we hear the horn, we'll know you got their attention. We'll get moving. That's all you have to do. Don't make them chase you any longer than necessary. Give up."

"I will," Nate promised. "And then I'll explain how I found this car in the woods with keys inside and took a little spin. Harmless youthful mischief."

"I doubt your parents will think so," Hannah said as if she had somehow found out why he was here in the first place. She turned to face Abdi. "How will we know you made it? That you're safe?"

"There will be no way to know until this is over. However, thanks to you, I have the number of General Towell in Tennessee. He is a good man. I am sure he will use his wise judgment and help me reach General Kane."

"I wish I could call General Towell and tell him to expect your call, but I think Nathan might be right. All phone calls in this area may be monitored."

"No matter," Abdi said. "I will convince him."

"Okay, your cousin knows to pick you up in an hour at the foot of the mountain on the other side, right?" Nate asked. The twins nodded, looking as though the reality of the situation was dawning on them. Nate checked his watch. "It's five to ten. Time we do this." Everyone stood. "Once we're out of here, wait at the bottom of the alcove," he told them. "Give me five minutes to get my grandparents into the front room, then you guys go out the back door."

Everyone filed up the ladder, each carrying a flashlight, and moved toward the door. Nate led the way and released the lock on the hideaway. He pushed the door open a crack and peeped out with more caution than ever. Deciding the coast was clear, he pulled the opening wide.

Icy blasts of air stung his skin as soon as he stepped out. He held up a hand to signal the others to wait and then moved back into the hideaway. Was Great-Gramps trying to tell him something?

A second bout of arctic air blew past. Nate pulled the opening almost close, certain something was wrong. He waited with his hands on the door, ready to close it fast if necessary.

In another moment, the muted sound of chaotic movements reached them. The china cabinet's entrance opened. His heart raced as he eased the door closed then pressed his back to the wall. He sent a silent thanks to Great-Gramps. They couldn't have made it back into the hideaway in time without the warning.

Nate motioned for the others to keep quiet and still as a pack of barking dogs entered the stairwell, followed closely by a rush of heavy footsteps storming up toward them.

The barks grew louder on the middle landing. Nate's heart skipped as he realized he had not bolted the lock. He switched the flashlight to his right hand and slowly moved the metal rod into place. Then he aimed his flashlight at the twins and Abdi and flipped it off, a signal for them to do the same.

They stood in complete blackness. Will's arm pressed against him, but neither moved a muscle. Nate thanked God that Abdi was last in line. If the dogs had Abdi's scent, maybe the three of them and the closed door of the hideaway would be enough to throw them off.

The search party lingered on the middle landing. Whimpers came from the dogs as they scratched against the wall that opened into the hideaway. Nate swallowed a rush of bitter saliva and a cold snake slithered in his guts.

Shuffling footsteps mingled with the sounds of scraping paws. Maybe two minutes passed and still the searchers' attention focused on the landing. Then finally, someone suggested the dogs must have lost the scent, and a loud burst of barking came as heavy steps stomped in waves up to the top. In a few seconds, the noise drew distant with the searchers moving to another part of the house. Nate wondered where his grandparents were and what they'd been told. Now he wished he had given them some warning.

His muscles ached from the stiffness and tension of keeping still. He decided to chance a peep at the stairwell to see if an agent had been left there. If someone spotted him, they were doomed. *Who am I kidding?* He reasoned. *We are doomed anyway.* Agents had to be all over the farm. Abdi making it to the woods was a long shot.

He undid the lock and opened the door enough to peep out. He didn't see anyone, but his line of sight was limited. He risked opening the door enough to stick out his head and checked both ways. No one guarded the stairs, but that did not mean no one guarded the door from the outside. He wondered what reason agents had to come back and search his grandparents' house and with dogs this time. As if they were certain Abdi was here. Nate backed into the hideaway. He flipped on his flashlight and signaled everyone to fallback.

"What are we going to do?" Hannah asked once they were deep in the hideaway again.

"What do you think happened to bring them back here?" Will asked. Abdi answered.

"I believe the USB may have activated a locator device when you put it into your computer," Abdi said. "I am sorry. I did not know until now it was fitted with such a tool."

"That explains it," Nate said. "If you guys still think we have a chance of pulling this off, we can try and sneak out the other way and hope for the best."

"What other way?" Hannah asked. "There's another exit out of here?"

"Yeah, it's there," Nate pointed to the plain looking wall behind her. "It opens inside the linen closet in my grandparents' bathroom. We may be able to slip into their bedroom from there and then out through the terrace."

"Then what are we waiting for?" Will said. "Let's do it."

Nate looked at him. "You guys aren't freaked?"

"Yeah, a little," Will said. "But my dad is buried at Arlington. I am not letting some toad-face plant of the Taliban get away with this."

"Ditto," Hannah said.

Nate turned to Abdi. "You know, this just got a lot more dangerous for you?"

"We proceed," said Abdi.

Nate could think of nothing to say. They had to know the odds as well as he, still they refused to give up. "Okay then. We go for it."

Abdi walked over to the wall and stooped. The door they needed to exit the hideaway blended perfectly with the wall like the ones in the secret stairway. Nate thought a hidden doorway, with a hidden latch, in a hidden hideaway was overkill, but Abdi opened it with no problem. They formed a line to transfer the content of towels and toiletries. Once they removed the shelves, Nate opened the linen closet door and entered the bath. He hoped all the agents had moved outside, but most likely one or two had been left to guard his grandparents. The best he could hope for was that most had moved to the yard.

He crawled out headfirst then stood and walked to the bathroom door. He stooped low to the floor before sticking his head into the bedroom to check for agents or his grandparents. He turned, feeling relieved the coast was clear and then saw that everyone had already come through the linen closet after him. He signaled for them to stay put as he stepped into the bedroom with caution.

Someone had left the overhead light on. He worried about being spotted from the window, but turning the light off might alert whoever maybe watching the house that they were inside. Two lanterns mounted on the terrace wall, glowed softly and showed no one standing watch outside.

He turned, heading for the kitchen to check for a guard. He took only a couple of steps before a fatigues-clad soldier filled the door to the bedroom, aiming an M4 rifle at his chest.

"What are you doing here, kid?" the soldier asked without lowering the weapon.

"Oh, I live here," Nate squeaked and raised both hands. "I mean, I'm visiting my grandparents for the summer."

"You're the grandkid? Where were you when we conducted the search?" the soldier asked, sounding suspicious.

"I just got back," Nate said. "I came through the backdoor. I was hanging out with some friends in the woods." He hoped the soldier hadn't been guarding the backdoor and knew he was lying.

"I've been in the kitchen," the soldier said. "How come I didn't see you come in?"

*Dang!* Nate couldn't think of an answer to the question. He swallowed and concentrated on keeping his eyes from the movement at the bathroom door. Hopefully the soldier didn't see it too. His mind raced, frantic for something to say that would keep the soldier's attention on him.

"Okay, yeah, I was afraid my grandparents were in there so I snuck in through the terrace." He pointed to the French doors behind him. "I'm not supposed to be out this late. They think I'm in my room," he explained, willing himself to shut up. Nothing gave away a lie faster than too much explanation.

The soldier kept the M4 rifle trained on him and pulled his collar towards his mouth. Nate realized he was about to speak into a microphone and give a report.

"Please, sir …" Nate started just as Abdi sprang from the bath-room with his 9mm drawn. The surprise attack worked to Abdi's ad-vantage. He used a roundhouse kick to knock the soldier's weapon from his hand. Then with lightning fast ninja speed, Abdi was on the man and gave him a chop against the neck that caused the soldier to crumble unconscious to the floor.

Abdi stuck his 9mm into his waistband at the small of his back and kicked the soldier's rifle into the bathroom. "Please find me something to secure him with," he said.

Nate ran to the pantry and grabbed a spool of gardening twine then returned to the bedroom and handed the spool to Abdi. He helped Abdi cut the twine into pieces with his pocketknife. Together they bound the soldier's hands and feet. Nate glanced up as they were securing the soldier to see Hannah and Will still inside the bathroom, looking as though they were in shock.

"We must hide him," Abdi said when they finished. "If they dis-cover him it will raise suspicion."

"Right." Nate looked to the twins. "Help us put him in the hide-away." The twins sprung into action like the mental bands holding them in place suddenly snapped. They helped dragged the soldier into the bathroom. It took several minutes to get about 200 pounds and six feet of dead weight into the hideaway through the narrow linen closet opening, but finally they succeeded.

They closed the opening without returning the content of the closet. Hopefully, no one would see the empty shelves. They chanced it, knowing they were running out of time. Everyone stood in the bathroom looking wide eyed; all aware the point of no return had been reached. Point one: a member of the United States army had been assaulted. Point two: the soldier had seen Abdi. And point three: now the plan had to work or they were in deep crap.

# 26
# GLITCHES

"Oh, we are so screwed." Everyone turned to stare at Hannah who blinked slowly and shook her head in disbelief. She returned their gazes and looked as though she wanted to shake some sense into them. "What?" she demanded. "We are!"

"Yeah, I know," Nate said. "But if you're talking like that, it must be worse than we think."

"How much worse can it get?" Hannah asked. "We assaulted a member of the armed forces, then we bound and hid him. I believe that qualifies as kidnapping. And guess what?" she asked, sounding on the verge of hysteria. "Kidnapping a serviceman in the pursuit of his duty is a federal offense!"

"She's right," Will said. "We're screwed."

"Do not worry," Abdi said. "He did not see you. If I am captured, I will tell them I held Nate Daniels hostage." Abdi looked at each of them with a calm assurance in his eyes. "It had to be done," he told them.

"He's right," Nate said. "We had to do it. Now we need to get past this. We need to carry on with the plan."

"There are no doubt other guards," Abdi said. "Will you do reconnaissance, Nate Daniels, and report back their location?"

"Yeah," Nate said. "But let's figure no one is in the kitchen, or he would have been in here by now. We don't have time to account for all their whereabouts. We need to make sure the key spots are clear: the backyard, the terrace, and the yard beyond that. Since they'll be expecting me to show up," he reasoned, "I won't look out of place if I walk out on the terrace and check out the area. If they see me, I'll just say what I told the soldier, but I shouldn't raise any red flags."

"You've already raised a red flag," Will reminded him. "They must already be suspicious. That soldier didn't exactly treat you like a possible victim. But none of us belongs here. I don't see any other way."

"Then you guys get back into the linen closet. I'll have a look out front and try to figure out what's going on. Don't come out 'til you hear me signal an all clear, got it?"

"Be careful, Nathan," Hannah said. She and the others returned to the bathroom then crawled on their knees through the hideaway opening. Nate walked across the room to the patio. He hoped he looked more relaxed than he felt.

He stepped through the door and walked to the iron rail surrounding the brick terrace. He rested his hands on the banister then took in a deep breath like he had come out for fresh air. Casually, he let his eyes roam the landscape, which was as black as ever. But if anyone was watchig him, they would be on him by now. *So where had they all gone?*

In a swift movement, he jumped over the railing and dropped to his knees behind a border of hedges surrounding the house. He crawled along the perimeter, carefully, peeping into every window he passed. In the library, he spied his grandparents sitting on the couch holding hands. Both General Jalapa and Special Agent Beckman were with them, holding a conference in front of the fireplace.

Nate's heart ached for his grandparents; they seemed so scared. He pushed down an impulse to get their attention to show he was all right. Instead, he continued around the house until he reached the front where he discovered dozens of cars parked on the driveway and lawn. It looked like a federal invasion.

He pulled back, pressing low against the house for cover. After a few seconds, he peered around the corner again. Wall-to-wall agents swarmed the front yard, seeming antsy. Like they were waiting for something. *But what? What's their next move?* Again Nate fell back to think about the meaning of a legion of anxious agents.

They already searched the house. Were they now planning on searching the woods? That made sense. If they picked up the signal from Abdi's USB, they were not going to wait for morning to start a search of the area. But maybe in their haste to get here, they hadn't prepared for the black Carolina night. They would need what? Night vision goggles and thermal imagery stuff?

Nate hurried back to the terrace and climbed over the rail and into the bedroom. He reached inside the linen closet and knocked four times. The concealed door opened and everyone filed out, looking expectantly at him.

"We can still make this work," he said, hurriedly. "But we don't have much time. Right now, they're all out front waiting for supplies, I think. It can come any minute now, and then they'll start to search the woods, so we need to hurry."

"Okay, let's go," Hannah said, looking anxious. "Nathan, which way is safe?"

"Out the back." Everyone moved to the kitchen with flashlights in hand.

Nate signaled the others to stay put as he opened the backdoor and stepped onto the porch. Within seconds, a soft rustling came from the pitch-black yard and a soldier stepped into a beam of light from the window. *Seriously?* At least this one didn't have a gun pointed at him.

"Hey," Nate said, trying to keep surprise out of his voice. "Is it okay if I hang here?"

"Where's Monroe?" the soldier asked.

"He's inside. He said it was cool for me to come out here."

"Hey, Monroe," the soldier called toward the still open door. When he didn't get an answer he looked at Nate suspiciously. "Wait there, kid." The soldier disappeared into the blackness before rays of light from the door found him again. He emerged from the shadows with his M4 raised, holding it in firing position.

"Oh yeah, I think he said he was going to the john," Nate lied. "Maybe that's why he didn't answer."

The soldier appeared doubtful. "Hold here 'til I check it out." Nate turned toward the door, intending to signal the twins and Abdi to take cover. But they were nowhere in sight.

The soldier reached the door and stepped around him. Standing in the doorway, he paused a moment and nudged Nate away from the entrance. A swell of guilt rose in Nate's throat. *He's pushing me out of line of fire,* Nate thought as he reached for the can of bear repellant on a shelf beside him.

"Monroe?" the soldier called as he strolled over casually to the bedroom. "You're supposed to tell me when you need to hit the head. You ever heard of protocol, dude?"

Nate eased into the kitchen quietly and kept a distance of about fifteen feet from the soldier. He kept his arm straight, with the hand holding the repellant just behind his thigh. Beyond the bedroom's entrance, the door to the bathroom was closed. Since Abdi and the twins were nowhere in sight, Nate assumed they were hiding there.

No answer from Monroe seemed to make the soldier even more suspicious. He glanced over his shoulder and spotted Nate. "Kid!" he said in a low exasperated whisper, jerking his head to the porch, "outside," he mouthed and jerked two fingers sharply toward the door.

"Yeah, but I'm sure everything's okay," Nate lied. *I'll be going to Hell with my mouth on fire.* The guy's only doing his job. "Do you want me to check out the bathroom? You can cover me if it makes you feel better." *Please say yes, please say yes,* Nate willed.

The soldier seemed torn between going over and physically putting him outside or continuing toward the bathroom. He must have decided the risk was minimal as he turned and stepped into the bedroom. "Monroe!" the soldier yelled. But another non-response caused the soldier's spidey senses to tingle. He raised his weapon high as he quickly approached the bathroom door, ready to fire.

*Oh crap,* Nate thought. He had to do something before the soldier moved out of range. "Excuse me, sir." The soldier turned, and Nate aimed a spray of repellent at his face.

Taken by surprise and fighting what had to feel like an inferno on his face, the soldier staggered back, off his guard. Nate dropped the can, ran over, and struggled with the soldier briefly before managing to wrestle the rifle over his head and out of his hands. Blinded and disoriented, the soldier stumbled to the floor.

"Sorry, man," Nate mumbled. "Really." He jumped away and opened the bathroom door. Abdi stood there with his gun drawn. Nate guessed Hannah and Will were inside the closet.

"We have another problem," Nate told Abdi, gesturing toward the man on the bedroom floor. "I had to mace him."

"I see," said Abdi. "We must tie him up as well."

Nate knocked four times on the closet to signal the twins to come out, then went over and took the spool of twine from the bedroom dresser.

Taking in the scene of a disabled soldier moaning and squirming on the floor with his hands covering his face, Hannah filled a paper cup with water from the bathroom tap. She walked over and tried to pour water over the soldier's eyes. "Let me help," she said as she pried the man's hands away.

"Hannah," Nate cautioned, "we don't have time. We need to tie him up."

Abdi took the man's rifle from Nate. "Help him stand," he told Nate and Will. "We must get him inside the hideaway quickly."

Hannah stroked the man's hair as if she was comforting a child with a boo-boo. Then she stepped away and allowed Nate and Will to lead the man inside the hideaway.

They worked fast as they bound the man's arms behind his back, and tied his legs together. Abdi studied the guy.

"He will be okay. Soon the affect of the spray will wear off. We must gag his mouth to prevent him from calling out. These two soldiers must not be found until after I am gone."

"Abdi is right," Nate agreed. He took a folded hand towel from the linen piled on the hideaway floor and twisted it into a coil. He forced the towel between the soldier's teeth then secured it with a tight knot. "Sorry," he mumbled again. "That does it," he told them. "We've lost a lot of time. We need to get moving"

Abdi opened the exit to the closet, and this time he led the way to the kitchen where, once again, Nate had everyone wait until he double-checked the coast was clear. He waited on the back porch for a minute before feeling sure no one else was watching. He beckoned the others out and waved them forward. Abdi, Will, and Hannah went down the porch steps and disappeared into the blackness of the lawn and the woods beyond.

Nate waited five minutes more, in order to give them enough time to get a head start before he initiated the most important part of the plan: get the attention of the agents and soldiers away from the woods and on him.

Confident that Abdi was far enough away, Nate ran into the wildflower meadows surrounding the lawn and kept low as he picked his way to where the dirt road started a quarter of a mile from the house. Once he reached the road, he ran faster along the smooth, unobstructed path. His distraction plan had to go into effect before the soldiers and agents got the equipment they needed to begin their search, otherwise it would be too late.

After moving far enough down the road to be out of sight, he straightened and ran even faster to cover the mile or so to the car. He came to a stop seven minutes later. Breathing hard, he swung a quick beam of light around to get his bearing. He was near the primordial woods. He hoped the flashlight wouldn't bring unwanted attention because he couldn't find the pipe bridge and the car without it.

Nate aimed his flashlight beam toward the ground, hoping his body would block it from being seen from the house. When he entered the woods, he swept the flashlight back and forth until he found the car.

Nate approached the car as he would a stick of lit dynamite, not completely sure an agent wasn't hiding somewhere nearby. A soldier popping out of nowhere to challenge him wouldn't surprise him a bit at this point. They were everywhere. But he reached the car without a problem. He felt both relieved and exhilarated as he climbed behind the wheel. He took the keys from above the visor, started the engine, locked the doors, and then turned the car and headed for the clearing.

# 27
# HERITAGE AND HONOR

The goal was to create a big enough distraction to ensure that agents wouldn't search the woods for another fifteen or twenty minutes. For that, Nate needed to get their attention.

He drove to the fork in the dirt road that led to the driveway and turned on the car's headlights. The agents swarming the yard took no notice of him. They probably assumed he was one of them. He needed to make them take a good look at Abdi's car. He held his position and revved the engine. Some agents glance his way but then turned away. None of them hopped in their cars to come after him. *What's wrong with these guys?*

He gunned the engine again and then tore through the meadows in front of his grandparents' house. In clear view of agents, he sped in circles, daring them to give chase.

He congratulated himself as some agents recognized the BMW and rushed to the field. Instead of going for their cars, the agents drew their guns. *Not good.* He decided it was time to scat and aimed the car back toward the dirt road. When the first bullet pierced the rear window, it took him a few moments to overcome the shock and realize he was being shot at. This did not fit in with his plan. They weren't supposed to want Abdi dead. *What idiot had given a shoot on sight order?*

Never had he considered this worst-case scenario: being shot at and maybe killed? He floored the gas and sped away. Suddenly, the chase had turned into something more than a game of decoy. He needed to stay alive.

Briefly, he considered getting out of the car and surrendering with his hands up, but he got a strong feeling that would be dangerous for his health. He wasn't Abdi, but they were about the same height and weight and even the same shade of brown. The agents would realize their mistake too late. This scenario meant he could not surrender.

Agents hopped into their cars in pursuit. A bullet grazed Nate's hand as it shot into the dashboard. A long narrow patch of his skin went bare before it filled with blood that quickly covered his hand.

He glanced over his shoulder in panic. Some inner Nate was jumping up and down inside his chest shouting, *Duck! Dodge! Duck! Dodge!* Then suddenly, cold air enfolded him like a blanket just before something punctured the back of the driver seat. He expected a bullet through his back, but amazingly, it didn't come. He took no time to consider this but floored the gas and met the road going 90 miles per hour.

Swerving and struggling to keep control of the car, he made a break for the rusty gate. Chunks of dirt spewed against the car as he forced the car even faster up the country road.

The agents chasing him were gaining ground. He pushed the peddle to the floor. If they caught him, at least one of the bullets that would riddle the car would find him, and he feared a second miracle might not come. Someone did not want Abdi alive to talk.

Nate fought back the panic roaring inside him and gasped for air. How would he make people listen to the truth? The odds of that were diminishing with every passing second. Now stopping to explain meant dying.

Rocks and dirt bounced off the car as he literally tore up the road. The gate was still a mile away. Where he needed to go from there he didn't know. How far he would get, he didn't know. All he knew was go, go, go!

At 160 miles per hour, the engine was firing on all cylinders. Another bullet singed the top of his head then exploded into the rearview mirror. He sent another silent thanks to Great-Gramps.

The gate had to be half a mile away now and he flew toward it. His best bet was to reach the highway where agents might hesitate to shoot in front of reporters. There would surely be reporters. *Please God, let there be reporters and no shooting in front of a national audience.*

He was maybe thirty yards from the gate when a Hummer pulled through on a collision course. He hit the brakes hard, causing the car to swirl off the road faster than he could regain control. He felt the car propelled into the air and saw a burst of white folding around him and then the BMW was rolling.

****

Half conscious, he felt grasping hands, lots of them, pulling him then moving him through the air. Suddenly, something hard and wet knocked against him. He was on his back and rain was falling. The last thing he remembered before slipping away was a woman's voice:

"Hold your fire! Hold your Fire! It's the kid!"

****

He woke from a weird dream to find his parents and Ell beside his bed. He smiled, and tried to speak; only his voice wouldn't work.

"Oh, you've been in an accident, honey," Mom told him. "You're in the hospital with a broken leg and a bad concussion. But you'll be fine."

"Bad dream," Nate tried to say, but nothing more than a weak puff of breath came from his mouth. He pointed at his throat.

"Yes, you've been unconscious for two days. Your throat is just dry. It probably hurts a little, and it's going to be hard for you to talk at first."

He looked at his dad who smiled. "Your mom has been pestering the nurses and doctors. She knows as much as they do by now." It occurred to Nate that maybe the car crash hadn't been a dream.

Ell piped up, "You're in *so* much trouble."

He smiled. *Yep, not a dream.* Everything that happened had been real. Strange, Mom and Dad were taking it amazingly well. But maybe it only seemed that way because of his head bump.

He looked at Ell and thought how much he had missed her, then remembered she had tried to tell him something before he left Boston. He wondered if she was ready to talk.

After a knocked at the door, Hannah walked in with his grandparents.

"There he is," Grandma said. "You gave us quite a scare, dear."

"We're sorry about that, Mama Ultima," Dad said. "We'll deal with Nate when we get him home."

*Really? Without hearing my side of the story? Come on, Dad.* He wished his voice would come back.

"Hi, Mr. and Mrs. Freedman," Hannah shook his parents' hands. "I'm very pleased to meet you. I want you to know Nathan had good reasons for what he did. He is so brave." Nate wanted to kiss her.

His mom looked skeptical. "We'll see about that."

*Okay*, he really needed his voice. "Ab…Abdi?" Nate managed to squeak. His throat burned like someone had poured sand down it.

Hannah took his hand and squeezed. "You'll see," she said, looking mischievous.

"So, who are you?" Ell asked, staring at the hand that Hannah held.

"Hi," Hannah released his hand and stuck her hand out to Ell. "Nate and I met on the plane. I'm his girlfriend."

"Girlfriend?" His mom and Ell said at the exact same moment. Nate's mouth upturned into a wide smile. *So, he officially had a girlfriend. Yes!*

"Wait …" Ell started to say something but was interrupted by Will walking into the room.

"I don't know why people complain about hospital food. I think it's delicious. We ought to come here for lunch sometimes," he said.

Ell turned, looking irritated for a moment before her gaze found Will and then her mouth dropped. She blushed, looked down and then up again with a dopey smile.

"William," Hannah said, "no one cares about your taste in food. You didn't even say hi to Nathan's family, and ..." Hannah looked at Ell whose pale complexion eliminated her from the family tree. "I'm sorry," Hannah said, "I didn't get your name."

"This is Elleana Rodriguez," Mom said. "Nate's best friend."

"Well, hello, Elleana." Will reached for her hand with a suave smile right out of a Will Smith movie. He held her gaze a moment and raised her hand to his lips.

"Hi," Ell said, looking goofy on top of dopey. The two just stood there like a stun ray had hit them. "So," Ell said, starting to bob up and down, "how do you know Nate?"

"Oh, through Han. I'm her brother."

"Really?" Ell said. "You know, I don't see the resemblance at all. Your features are totally different."

"Well, of course we're fraternal twins," Hannah said. "So one wouldn't expect much similarity."

"Twins?" Ell questioned. "Boy, you would never guess. I mean. Looking at her, then looking at you."

"Wait, what?" Hannah said, seeming to take the statement as an insult. "What does that mean?"

"Yeah, well, Han is sensitive about her looks," Will said, looking as goofy as Ell. "We try not to mention it."

"Now look—" Hannah started before Will interrupted.

"So you're Nate's best friend? Has he been keeping you posted on what we've been doing?"

"No," Ell said, smiling a gaga smile. "Nate hasn't even called me since he's been here."

*Which has been all of seven days,* Nate thought. *What's up with these two?*

"Jeez, Elleana," Will said, "looks like you need to find yourself a new best friend."

"Yeah, I'm sure you're available," Nate's voice came in a hoarse crack, and it felt like hot lava lined his throat. "But Ell and I are fine."

"Yeah?" Will released Ell's hand with a wink then took a backpack off his shoulders. "They said you'd be in the hospital for another day, so I brought you something to read." He reached inside and pulled out Nathan Freedman's journal. "You didn't tell us you found this."

"Sorry." Nate put a hand to his throat like it would help soothe the burn. "So much was going on. Have you read it?"

"A lot of it," Will said. "Want to hear?"

"Sure," Nate welcomed anything that kept him from being the one talking. "Tell us what you know." His mom handed him a styrofoam cup of crushed ice with a spoon in it from the bedside table.

Will pushed Nate's good leg aside and made himself comfortable at the foot of the bed. "Well, Nathan Freedman was born a slave, but he was the son of the plantation's owner. Growing-up, he showed a talent for designing buildings. That impressed his father. So, he was allowed privileges denied other slaves. For instance, he was secretly taught to read. He caught on quickly to the things the slave builders taught him. He was eleven when he started building dollhouses for plantation owners' daughters. At sixteen, he was designing and building his signature houses." Will stopped to shake his head. "I can't even imagine," he said, sounding awed. "That's just a year older than we are." He looked at Ell and flashed another smile before he continued.

"At twenty-one, Nathan Freedman's father let him buy his freedom, but at a price low enough to be considered a gift. Nathan tried to use the money he saved to buy the freedom of a girl he loved, Ana, but her owner refused to sell her. Nathan was forced to leave her behind."

"Wait," Mom interrupted, looking confused. "Where are you getting this information?"

"Nathan Freedman left a journal," Nate told her. The ice was making his throat better.

"Abdi told us about the journal," Hannah said. "We found it in Nate's room the morning after the crash."

"Abdi?" his mom questioned. "Hideaway?"

"Yeah," Nate said. "I'll tell you everything, but can we hear this part first?"

Mom looked at Dad, who said, "Continue, please."

"Well," Will said, "he intended to come back for Ana, but he waited too long. It took five years to get established. By the time, he thought he'd done well enough to support Ana in style, she had been sold to another plantation and no one knew where.

"That's when he decided to move south. He was a mulatto, so he was tolerated more than someone with darker skin. He built a house and continued his search while trying to appear as though he embraced the antebellum culture.

"He went from plantation to plantation looking for Ana. He had taught her to read, so he peppered the plantations with the type of note Nate found."

"So how did a note end up in the mantel?" Nate asked.

"Maybe he kept one where it could be easily reached, but missed during a search. But I guess we'll never really know," Will said.

"Did he find Ana?" Hannah asked.

"Nope."

"Then he's still looking for her," Nate said.

Hannah looked at him like she though he must be still confused from the concussion. "He can't still be looking for her, Nathan. He's been dead for nearly one hundred and fifty years. But isn't it romantic how his love for her kept him in the South. And he became a station master hoping she would show up at his door," Hannah said. "That's love."

His mom looked wonderingly at the three. "What have you kids been up to?"

"Long story, Mom," Nate said. "But I promise I'll explain."

"We've already heard most of the story from Hannah and William," Grandma said. "But we didn't say anything because we thought you should hear it from Nathan."

Hannah checked her watch and jumped up and down with a squeal. "It's time, it's time!!!" she said and flipped the TV to MSNBC and turned up the volume.

**"HE'S BEING CALLED A NATIONAL HERO,"** news commentator Brian William's voice boomed from the set. **"In a surprising turn of events, accused terrorist Abdul Ahmead, who turned himself in twenty-four hours ago, is now being dubbed a hero. Mr. Ahmead, who worked undercover for three years as a plant in the**

Taliban army, delivered solid evidence of a planned military ambush orchestrated by a top general at the Pentagon. In a few moments, General Kane will broadcast live from the Pentagon with details of this foiled terrorist plot."

Nate's face turned into a giant grin. *Abdi made it!*

"Look, look!" Hannah squeaked. "Abdi is with the general!" Sure enough, Abdi stood in the background as a general walked to a podium and begin to elaborate on the planned ambush attack.

"Go, Abdi," Nate croaked.

The general rehashed what the newsman had said. But each time reporters asked for more details, General Kane cited national security. The general finished by praising Abdi's patriotism. Still, Abdi looked pained to be there, which fit with the Abdi Nate knew. Not one to go for the limelight, they must have twisted his arm to get him to appear. Then Abdi did something even more amazing. He asked the general if he could say a few words. The general shook Abdi's hand and took a step back as the world listened.

**"I could not have accomplished this without the help of Nate Daniels, who is a descendant of a station master of the historical Underground Railroad. Also, my gratitude to William and Hannah Greathouse, whose father lies among the Honored Dead in Arlington."** Abdi looked directly into the camera as though he knew they were watching. **"Thank you. I am forever in your debt."** He bowed, and it seemed there wasn't a sound in the world until he lifted his head once more.

**"That was Abdul Ahmead who is being called a hero after a three-day manhunt that cumulated in the shocking arrest of General Jalapa ..."** Hannah flipped off the TV, brushing a tear from her eye.

"Wow," Nate said.

His mom turned from the set to stare at him. "Young man, you need to do some fast talking."

**THE END**

# Author's Notes

North Carolina, in a vendetta against public support for emancipation, passed the 1830 Proclamation, which ordered all Blacks emancipated after that year to leave the state. This law did not necessarily apply to previously emancipated Blacks. In truth, at any given time during the course of slavery, ten percent of North Carolina's Black population was free. Hence, the writer has taken a creative liberty here.

The poetry of the fictional Nathan Freedman was inspired by words from the song, *Follow the Drinking Gourd*. Unlike Freedman's poem, the *Drinking Gourd* was not written, but sung in the tradition of many African nations where songs relayed many kinds of information.

It may interest the reader to know that the song *Sweet Chariot* is a Negro spiritual once sung often in the hot fields of a plantation. The verses hid a coded message. It alerted any slave with a mind to run for freedom that a conductor was on the premises and waiting to offer assistance.... *A band of angels coming after me. Coming for to carry me home.*

I humbly dedicate this book to all the angels we never knew.

In *The Last Station Master*, some prominent members of the Underground Railroad were mentioned. You may be wondering who they were. Read on to find out.

## JOHN PERCIAL PARKER

Soil Pulverizer                    Portable Screw Press

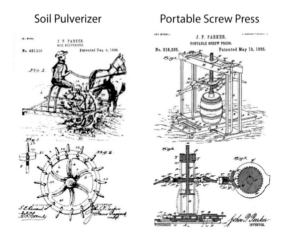

## EX-SLAVE, CONDUCTOR, ENTREPRENEUR, INVENTOR.

In 1827 John P. Parker was born to a slave mother and a white father in Norfolk, Virginia. At eight, John was broken hearted to be sold by his father to a plantation in Mobile, Alabama. Over the years, John's heartache grew into anger and resentment as he worked to save enough money to buy his freedom. It took eighteen years, but finally John put away enough money to free himself. He moved to Cincinnati, Ohio, where he met his wife, Miranda. Later they moved to Ripley, Ohio, and settled down to live a quiet life, or so it seemed.

In Ohio, John met a minister named John Rankins who was deeply involved in the Underground Railroad movement. Through the minister, John found a way to vent his anger and frustration against slavery. By day John appeared to be no more than a hard worker, forging iron for a living. However, by night, John made frequent trips to the neighboring slave state of Kentucky where he led hundreds of slaves to Canada and freedom.

Soon the elusive conductor's actions sparked a thousand-dollar bounty for his capture. John escaped many times by the thinnest of margins after having been beaten-up or shot at. Never giving up,

John continued his raids into slavery territory, and when the Civil War broke out in 1861, he helped recruit for an all-black regiment.

After the Civil War, John opened a foundry and machine shop. A brilliant man, John patented many types of agricultural equipments such as a screw for tobacco presses and the Parker Soil Pulverizer. John died a wealthy man and his foundry continued well after his death in 1900, only closing in 1918. John Parker's autobiography, *His Promise Land*, was published in 1998.

## PEG-LEG JOE and the Drinking Gourd

One of the most mysterious figures in Underground Railroad lore is the legendary Peg-Leg Joe. Who he was depends on whom you ask. Some say an ex-slave who escaped to the North only to return again and again to lead others to freedom. Others say he was a white sailor who hired himself out to plantation owners as a handyman. The one thing everyone agrees on is that Joe traveled the South, singing a coded song that mapped a way to freedom. In the spring, Peg-Leg Joe would return to the plantations he had visited to serve as conductor to all who heeded his message.

### Lyrics to the Drinking Gourd

When the Sun comes back
And the first quail calls
Follow the Drinking Gourd,
For the old man is a-waiting for to carry you to
freedom
If you follow the Drinking Gourd

The riverbank makes a very good road.
The dead trees will show you the way.
Left foot, peg foot, travelling on,

Follow the Drinking Gourd.

The river ends between two hills
Follow the Drinking Gourd.
There's another river on the other side
Follow the Drinking Gourd.

When the great big river meets the little river
Follow the Drinking Gourd.
For the old man is a-waiting for to carry you to
freedom
If you follow the Drinking Gourd

**Interpreting the song:** The first verse tells the runaway to leave in spring. The old man in the verse is believed to be Peg-Leg Joe himself.

In the second verse, Joe advises the runaway to follow the Tombigbee River and look for dead trees, which Joe would mark with the drawing of a peg leg. In addition to that, the river bank helped to throw off tracking dogs that could not pick up scent in water.

In the third and fourth verses Joe tells the runaway to watch for the Tennessee River (little river), which would eventually meet up with the Ohio River (the big river) where a conductor would lead them on to Canada and freedom.

Unfortunately, we may never know anymore about Peg-Leg Joe than his dedication to helping slaves find freedom. Where he came from and where he died are secrets as mysterious and as deep as who he really was.

**\*\*\*Check out** http://www.northern-stars.com/Follow_theDrinking_Gourd.pdf to learn more about Peg-Leg Joe and his Drinking Gourd. Courtesy of The Northern Planetarium, 15 Western Ave., Fairfield Maine 04937

## HARRIET TUBMAN: THE BLACK MOSES

If ever the phrase 'looks can be deceiving' applied to anyone, then it applied to Harriet Tubman. William Still, the black station master, described her as: *"A woman of no pretensions, indeed, a more ordinary specimen of humanity could hardly be found among the most unfortunate-looking farm hands of the South. Yet, in point of courage, shrewdness and disinterested exertions to rescue her fellow-men ... she was without her equal."*

Born between 1820 and 1822 in Dorchester County, Maryland as Araminta Ross, Harriet spent her childhood and young adult life as a slave. At twenty-five, she was permitted to marry a free black man, John Tubman, and later took her mother's first name.

When the owner of the plantation died, Harriet feared that she and her family would be split up and sold to work on chain gangs. She and two of her brothers decided to run away; however, in route her brothers soon became disenchanted with the notion and turned back. Faced with the task of accomplishing a feat rarely conquered by a woman alone, Harriet beat the odds and reached Pennsylvania and freedom.

Harriet was not satisfied with her own freedom. She returned to the South to help others to escape, including her seventy-year old parents. Despite having a $40,000 bounty on her head, Harriet returned to the south nineteen times and led over three hundred people to freedom.

When the Civil War started, Harriet became a spy for the Union Army, risking more forays into Southern territory. After the war, Harriet settled in Auburn, New York, where she died in 1913.

## WILLIAM STILL: Father of the Underground Railroad

Because of his family's tragic history with slavery, William Still devoted his life to aiding runaway slaves find their way to freedom. His father, Levin, had bought his own freedom but left his wife and four children behind. William's mother later ran away with the children and made it to freedom. Sadly, she and the children were caught and returned to Maryland and slavery. Undaunted, his mom made the heart-wrenching decision to run for freedom again, but this time, she would leave the oldest two boys behind. On her second try, she reunited with her husband. She changed her name from Sydney to Charity, and then the family changed their surname from Steel to Still. William was born 1821, fourteen years later. He grew up knowing the deep toll slavery had taken on his family.

William left home as a young man of twenty. Three years later he married his wife Letitia George and found work as a janitor with the Pennsylvania Society for the Abolition of Slavery. Soon, William became involved with the organization's anti-slavery movement. He helped create the finest network of safe houses and conductors around. William kept extensive records on the runaways he aided to help families find each other and to document their heroic efforts to obtain freedom.

During the Civil War, William gave up his post with the abolitionist society and started a business selling stoves and coal. Successful and smart, William grew wealthy and sponsored many charities throughout the course of his life.

In 1872 William self-published, *The Underground Railroad*, his journal account of his time as a station master and conductor. The book also included stories he collected from runaways. Once commonly known as the father of the Underground Railroad, William died in 1902 from a heart condition.

# A Short Glossary

**Black Codes** – A list of codes that governed the rights, or lack thereof, of freed Blacks and slaves. This book was based on the codes passed by North Carolina in 1830, however most Southern states had such a code. Many thanks to the North Carolina Department of Digital History. http://www.learnnc.org/lp/editions/nchist-antebellum/5328

**Conductor** – The men and women who operated the Underground Railroad and 'conducted' escaped slaves along the route to freedom.

**Emancipation Proclamation** – President Abraham Lincoln issued the Emancipation Proclamation on January 1, 1863. It stated that all persons held as slaves within the rebellious areas were to henceforward be free.

**Forwarding** – The transfer of run-a-ways from one safe house to another.

**Guantanamo Bay** – Located in Cuba, President George Bush established Guantanamo detention camp in 2002 for detainees of the war in Afghanistan. Later detainees from Iraq were placed there as well.

**The Henrietta Marie** – The oldest slave ship ever excavated. After delivering her 'cargo' of approximately 200 slaves to Jamaica in the seventeen hundreds, the Henrietta Marie restocked with supplies of sugar, cotton, and indigo to trade back in Britain. But as the ship approached the Florida Keys, bad weather and the New Ground Reef claimed the ship and all her crew. Three hundred years later, starting in the 1980's and continuing into the 1990's, scientists began excavating and conserving rescued items as a way to gain insight into life aboard a slave ship.

**Station Master** – The keeper of the safe house or station.

**The Underground Railroad** – A vast network of people who helped fugitive slaves escape to the North as well as Canada. It was not an actual railroad. It is believed that the term was adopted when a runaway being chased by a white mob and a pack of dogs disappeared near a river bend. The owner was heard to say, "It's as if he disappeared into an underground railroad." The name stuck. The backbone of the Underground Railroad was the many black and white conductors, safe houses, and station masters that moved the 'cargo' along. Usually, knowledge of the railroad was limited to a need to know basis. Often, members of the local UGRR only knew their members and not the overall operation. Each year, hundreds of slaves were aided. Between 1810 and 1850 it is estimated that between 60,000 and 100,000 slaves found their way to freedom.

## Credits and Sources

1. John P. Parker, **His Promised Land**: The Autobiography of John P. Parker, Former Slave and Conductor on the Underground Railroad, Publisher: W.W. Norton & Company, 1998, Print
2. William Still, **The Underground Railroad**: A Record of Facts, Authentic Narratives, Letters, &c., Narrating the Hardships, Hair-Breadth Escapes and Death Struggles of ... & Others or Witnessed by the Author. A Public Domain Book, Published 1872, Digital
3. Sarah H. Bradford, **Harriet, the Moses of her People**. Publisher: MacMay Publishing, 2008, Digital

Portraits and drawing used in accordance with the statue regulating Public Domain.

# About the Author

S.A.M. Posey lives in Florida with her family, a beagle, and a calico cat. Among her many ways of passing time, writing is her favorite. *The Last Station Master* is her debut novel.

You can learn more about the author and contact her through her web page at: www.samposey.com